ELEANOR'S TRAINING

Erik D. Astor

ELEANOR'S TRAINING

4PLAY PRESS

Motivational Knife Coach Aaron assures Brett that after only eight weekends of his program Brett's wife Eleanor will return less inhibited, more open sexually, and a libido that will wear him out. Aaron doesn't reveal she will also return home a slut and a whore.

Prologue

I am walking down Orient Beach in St. Martin, it is a beautiful sunny day, and the view is spectacular, because 25 meters in front of me is a beautiful long haired brunette. She is still pale, a light brown that is evident she has been in a tanning booth prior to arriving here, the way women do to not get burned beet red on their first few days on the vacation beach. Apparently, she has not been on the island long.

The sun is gleaming off her thin coating of suntan oil, coconut based. I am close enough behind her to still catch the hint of it in the air. her black hair is pulled back and held with a scrunchie. She is barefoot. And wearing nothing other than the dark sunglasses over her eyes. She is carrying a swimsuit cover of some sort in her left hand.

The woman appears about five foot six or seven inches, 128 or so pounds, in shape. Her pert ass is flexing with each step, her long legs are moving in a steady stride, gracefully, almost gliding. The indention of the muscle on the side of her thighs shows with each step. She walks taller, erect, shoulders back, her ample breasts thrust out, bouncing with each step, and she walks proudly, confident. While she is pretty, in shape, her air of confidence makes her more appealing and sexier. Her broad smile to those that pass her light up her face, giving off both sexiness and an air of approachability.

Men notice, they follow her with their eyes. Further ahead, 100 meters or so I see three young black men staring, talking among themselves, and the bolder of the three stands, his hair in long dreads, dark black, an assured smile, and he stands, glances back to his friends with a "watch-this" toss of his head, and turns down the beach toward the beautiful woman walking up the beach.

As an observer of people, I see a collision of sorts as they near. Not one of physical collision, but a mental fender bender. She slows and turns at times, looking behind her, surveying the beach or the ocean, in those half turns is when I see her smile, and the outline of a beautiful ample pair of breasts.

She is buck naked, as is the black man approaching. He is sporting a long uncut cock, exceptionally thick, swinging with his steps.

I'm close enough by now to hear her say, "Bonjour".

He sounds Jamaican. "Hey, you are one fine looking Momma," he says, turning to walk beside her. They walk faster, more animated, walking out of my hearing, but their conversation is animated.

The beautiful woman laughs, the young black man smiles. He says something and she shakes her head no, and he points to a bar with red umbrellas and chaise lounges. She nods, says something else, and by now they are approaching his two friends. He peels off to return to them, smiling. They give him a high five, he says something to them, and they laugh in obvious congratulations of some achievement.

The woman in front waves to the three black men, again a peal of laughter, and she parades on, still smiling, her back a bit straighter, thrusting her breasts out proudly, but a different sort of smile. A nice sway to her tight ass. She half turns and sees me closing.

In my hand is a long silver chain, designed to go around a woman's waist. She stops and I approach her. I reach out with the chain. "May I?" I ask. "You appear under dressed."

I reach around her waist, snap it so that it hangs at an enticing angle from her waist at an angle toward her hip.

"I wondered where you went," she said.

"The vendor down the beach, I stopped to haggle. This looked like you," I said.

"It is nice, thank you."

"Happy anniversary," I said. "Who's your new friend?"

"A very personable young man with confidence, good taste in the woman he approaches, and a nice thick cock," she said.

"And?"

"He invited me to join him for a drink around 6. He was very convincing."

"What did you tell him?" I asked.

"What do you think I would tell him," she says with a half-smile and a glint in her eye. "I said I would, did you see the cock he is packing?" she says, pausing, "you are invited as well."

"He knows that I am your husband?"

9

"No, but you can sit back and watch the play, or we can lay out the guidelines on how we play, however you would like to play it," she says.

"It is your anniversary, why don't you play it the way you would like," I offered.

"It is your anniversary too. Why don't we play it by ear," she said. I laughed.

"Why are you laughing?"

"I think I can predict how this is likely to end," I said.

"I've never fucked a Jamaican before," she says, as if the summation of her reasoning.

"That's my wife, can't take her anywhere," I joke.

"Hey, you are the one that brought me here, remember."

"I love you," I smile.

"I love you too," she says, taking my hand, and we continued up the beach, holding hands with the beautiful naked woman who is stopping conversations as we continue.

I think back to less than a year ago, when this woman I am holding hands with was a modest, conservative prim and proper woman, with no confidence in her appearance, too shy to speak to strangers, and who became offended if I even hinted at her fucking someone else outside of brief moments during role play.

We came to this same beach a year earlier, where after much convincing Eleanor stripped nude, but balked at sitting up and adamant that she was not going to walk nude down the beach with me. No way.

Much can change in a year I thought, as she half turns to me and I catch the sun gleams off a thin gold bar neatly piercing each nipple.

Actually the change took place over only eight weekends. My wife was trained by the first man to fuck her outside our marriage.

Chapter 1

Eleanor and I attended the wedding of a favorite niece in Lakeland, Florida. We were at the reception, bored, seeking relief in copious amounts of wine, so much that I was lightheaded. Eleanor was enjoying a great buzz, smiling her silly smile and giggling a giggle that lasts a little longer than normal.

I was looking to the dance floor, where at that moment my intoxicated wife was tightly pressed against the body of our new friend, Aaron, who by chance had ended up at our table at the crowded reception. I could not hear what they were saying, but she was buying into it all, responding, smiling, nodding, looking into his eyes. I saw Aaron's his hand slide down to her ass, caress for a second and pull her lower body even tighter against his. Our most recent tiff had been over her still trying to be the upstanding prim and prudish example for our children, even though both were off to university.

Uncharacteristically, Eleanor did not resist Aaron's grope and seemed to be enjoying the attention, no resistance, melding her body against his. I was not expecting this, and did not react, but then again, as young empty nesters, we are rediscovering ourselves, and as Eleanor said when we left to head to this wedding, "Our children are out of the house, now it is our turn," and I had challenged her to prove it. I thought her dancing with Aaron was my payback,

one of those, "If that is what you want watch this."
She thought she was calling my bluff.

***

It was February and still cold in our small-town
north of Atlanta, the weather there was lousy and
rainy since Christmas. Any excuse to drive to sunny
Florida, even for a wedding that time of year was a
godsend. We jumped at the chance.

I had a secondary reason. Eleanor and I married
right out of high school, had our kids early, and had
been empty nesting since September, when our
youngest left for college. I believed a trip might start
the thawing of her icy exterior. As usual, I was
waiting/hoping for the smoldering hot woman I knew
lurked inside her to emerge. Despite my gentle
pushing I saw no signs at home other than her words,
"It is our turn now."

Eleanor is something of a weight obsessive gym
rat, and blessed with spectacular genes, so much in
fact that it is common for strangers to mistake
Eleanor as a big sister to our daughters rather than
their mother. She loves when that happens. Although
she is 39, when someone asks how old she is she says
first, "A woman that will tell you that will say
anything." If they persist, she asks next, "Hold old do
you think I am?" The answer is always 33 to 35.
Eleanor will smile and say, "Close enough."

I get a rush from having a trophy wife without
the typical expense. I have witnessed several of my
friends delve into a midlife crisis: a nasty divorce and

13

tossing the first wife aside for the younger hot No. 2. A second wife is often very expensive. I was spared that. I found my trophy wife early and hung on, and as she matured, she grew even more beautiful and graceful. She maintained her youthful figure, and learned more about make-up, accents, dressing well, although her modesty always kept her from displaying her exceptional body, almost to the point of prudish.

I have always wanted her to open more, get rid of some of her modesty. With my prodding she attended a local modeling school but gave up any attempt at modeling after working as a hostess at a couple of car shows. "That's not me," she said.

It is still a wonderful life though, with the kids gone it's easier to have drinks by the pool, get frisky and feely out there without worrying about interruption, and go inside for raucous humping whenever the feeling strikes, but I would still like her to let others she the sultry sexy side of my wife she keeps hidden.

***

That is not to say that rediscovering each other even after 20 years together is not an adjustment. I had spent many of those first 20 years concentrated on work. Eleanor spent much of that time as working her bookkeeping job and raising children. My small leasing and rental company grew to the point I had a good staff to which I could delegate the day to day and take more time off, Eleanor had advanced in her

14

department store job that she had no issue with shifting to part time, allowing us much more time together.

Our first trip in this new segment of our lives was in December, to St. Martin, fleeing the cold, but I bore an overriding desire to do something new and exciting, something we had never done before, go to a nude beach, Eleanor reluctantly agreed.

On the beach I rolled over on my stomach to conceal my erection the first time Eleanor removed her top on the public beach. Yes, there were plenty of other women around us topless, but this was Eleanor, my wife, displaying her bare breasts in public. After a lot of encouragement from me, it took her until the second day to build up the courage to remove her bikini bottom, and only then after carefully trimming her pubis shorter and narrower. I heaped praise on her, the vacation sex was off the wall. She refused to stand and walk down the beach nude though.

"Next time," I told her.

"Bring me back here again and maybe we will see about it," was all she promised. It wasn't a no.

Chapter 2

The wedding reception bar was open and lavish trays of canapes were passed around while the wedding party was taking their wedding photographs. Eleanor and I took our wine and small plates to a table toward the back of the room. Many of those in the front near the dance floor had reserved signs on them for the immediate family, forcing the other wedding guests to crowd the few remaining tables.

We were seated at a six-person round table, with three older overweight women in loud print dresses and equally loud voices commandeered the three chairs on my side, when a tall distinguished looking man with salt and pepper hair dressed in a hand-tailored suit approached and asked permission to sit, so we invited him to join us.

The three women beside me had scooted their chairs closer together and were in their own world, leaving Eleanor and I to talk to our guest, who introduced himself to us as Aaron, and thanked us for allowing him to join us, as he knew very few people here. Thus, began the usual get to know you exchanges. Where are you from? He lived south of Macon but was in Atlanta regularly on business. How do you know the wedding couple? The groom is the son of an old friend and onetime neighbor, who was now deceased. In a courteous deep baritone voice, he explained that his wife was deceased, he had absorbed himself into his business of personnel and motivation consulting, which had been growing rapidly, thanks to an infusion of cash from his wife's life insurance policy. He had recently decided it was time for less work and more smelling the roses. He gave Eleanor a warm smile, checking her out with his piercing pale blue eyes. I have long been accustomed to men checking out my wife, although she never really notices.

"Such as the delight of have a beautiful woman allowing me to sit at her table," he said, giving a slight bow of her head as he said it. I thought it overdramatic, but it was clear Eleanor loved it.

"Thank you, I'm glad you think so," Eleanor said.

More drinks and questions, his turn, where we told him of our children in college, a few months into our empty nesting, and we too had determined to spend less concentration on work and more on enjoying our successes. His easygoing manner and melodic voice adding to his attentive listening had us both opening more than usual to a stranger.

"To success," Aaron said, raising our glasses to his, "And the time to enjoy it."

The conversation drifted to his occupation, analyzing and developing motivational projects for top echelon officers at major bases, the Pentagon, and U. S. Embassies on a government contract, as well as life coach and motivational oriented smaller civilian projects. The job required a lot of travel in the past, but he was concentrating more on domestic work now.

"Oh, that would be so exciting," Eleanor said. "I've always wanted to travel. I hope we can start

17

doing more of that," she said with a sideways glance to me. Aaron was soon regaling us with entertaining stories of being stranded in the desert of Africa with a broken-down car, leaving a bar minutes before a terrorist bombing, the exotic South Pacific out of the way places accessible only in a dugout canoe, and even a tourist trip to the Antarctic. He was American but his travels gave him a continental air.

The band started, playing at a volume too loud for conversation as the groom, bride and rest of the wedding party entered in a boisterous flurry and began dancing and drinking began in earnest.

Eleanor loves to dance much more so than me, although I had taken enough ballroom dance lessons with her to learn a few basic steps like a foxtrot. She had continued for a couple of months longer, knew more dances than me, and had a natural talent for it, and she enjoys it. My lack of interest is a frustration for her, that I did not hold her same enthusiasm.

It was not a surprise when another song started and she wanted to dance, and I begged off. Seeing that Eleanor wanted to dance, Aaron asked my permission before extended his hand to her. As I expected he turned out to be an elegant dancer, and they made a striking pair. Eleanor was enjoying herself, laughing, twirling, smiling, exchanging glances and whispers, dancing through three fast songs and then one slow waltz. I watched her animated facial movements, she was locked on his face, enjoying the conversation as they glided across the dance floor like Fred Astaire and Ginger Rogers. I wasn't jealous of the attention Aaron was receiving.

He was entertaining my wife, she was enjoying it, dancing, something I did not like to do. I was thankful for the help.

I looked up and Eleanor and Aaron were walking back to our table, she was still holding her hand. That felt strange. I had never seen her holding hands with another man before. They returned to the table after the 4th dance.

"Thank you, that was delightful," Eleanor said, "Please excuse me for a moment." She left to the restroom and Aaron took his seat.

"You don't like to dance, I take it," he said.

"No, more like a chore for me, glad you are able to fill in," I said.

"More than happy to," Aaron said, "Any time I am able to dance with a gorgeous woman it makes it a delightful day. We all get too few of those." He gave me a warm smile. "You do know how lucky you are to be married to a beautiful vivacious woman like Eleanor don't you? Has she modeled? She has the look."

"I married up," I smiled, "And yes, I do know it, but no to the modeling, she went to modeling school but after a couple of gigs decide it was just not something she wanted to continue."

Eleanor was interrupted on her way back to our table by a young man in his late 20's asking her to dance. She gave me a questioning look and I nodded a go-ahead with a smile, and the two of them moved to the dance floor. I lost them in the crowd.

Aaron was studying me, scooting over into Eleanor's chair. "You know, I've always enjoyed trying to figure people out, look for indicators on what they do versus what they say, what is really in the back of their minds. I assume you notice the inner glow that exudes from your wife. Almost like an aura?"

I had no idea what Aaron was talking about and told him so.

Before I could ask him to explain, Eleanor came to the table, gushing. "Wow," she said, "Did you see me? That guy I was dancing with, when he asked me to dance, I told him I had shoes older than him, but he insisted, he told me he is intrigued with beautiful older women." Eleanor giggled, evidence of both she enjoyed the attention, and the wine was hitting harder. "He even asked me for my phone number," she laughed.

"That should be an ego boost," I said.

"Well earned," Aaron said.

"Did you give it to him?" I asked, teasing, but she glared at me.

"Don't make fun of me."

"I'm sure he wasn't," Aaron said, saving the moment. "Your husband sees that the young man only did what every man in this room wants to do," he smiled. She still kind of glared at me. Eleanor had consumed enough wine that she was in that two-drink, get-mean phase, that should pass once the third glass hit her.

Again Aaron, as if sensing the tenseness looked at me and asked again, "May I?" Again, I nodded, and he took Eleanor back to the dance floor. The lights had dimmed, and the band was going into a set

20

of more slow songs, and I was getting more into drinking, as the waiters seemed to have made it a mission to keep my glass full. In my mind free drinks are the only good thing about attending someone else's wedding.

After several dances Aaron and Eleanor returned to the table, and she was clearly on a high that wasn't only because of the wine but also from the attention she was receiving. I did not know exactly what Aaron was saying to her, but she was clearly enjoying it. Their conversation at our table was interrupted twice by friends of Aaron bringing other woman to him for an introduction, one very pretty, young, with long blonde hair and another willowy young woman with a chop cut red hair and upper arm tats of flowers and butterflies.

I sized it up quickly, Aaron being unmarried, a female friend of his was trying to hook him up with the other two women, neither wearing wedding rings, I noted, likely both divorced and his female friend seeing Aaron as therapy for the young divorcees.

Aaron was polite but quickly brushed them off, returning all his attention and charm back on my wife Eleanor. I felt like I was standing outside their zone, the way they were concentrating on each other. It felt strange.

Again, she excused herself for the bathroom, and again the same young man from before stopped her on the way back, and for a second time she let him lead her to the dance floor, where they embraced in a slow dance. I was watching with rapt attention, not so much as to police any advances of the young man,

21

but for another reason, and that was watching my wife's attention and flirting with him so blatantly, and how she pressed her body into his as they danced. She was teasing him with her body for sure, something uncommon for her.

Aaron watched and looked back at me again. "Amazing, isn't it?"

"What?"

"How erotic it can be when someone else is flirting and paying attention to your wife. It is clear he wants her. Of course, there are many in this room that want her, look around, look at the faces following her." I did, and he was right, there were at least nine or ten men off to the side staring at my wife. "She enjoys the attention, she likes to flirt," he said.

"Yes."

"Does that bother you? Make you jealous? Or do you get off on other men wanting your wife? That's not uncommon, you know."

"I know how desirable she is, probably more than she knows herself. Truth is I like her getting the attention, it makes me proud she is mine. She enjoys the flirting, so we're good."

"Do you think she's been totally faithful?" Aaron asked. "A beautiful woman like that gets hit on all the time, sometimes in front of you, doesn't she? Has she ever been tempted? There are so much that women don't tell us." I started to say he was butting into things that were none of his business, but he said it so softly, sincerely, that the question did not seem like

22

an intrusion, but one of sympathetic understanding. I opened up.

"Yes, she gets hit on a lot. She is faithful. I have confidence in that." Aaron gave me a smug smile.

"But do you suppose she has ever wanted to? Has she thought and wondered about it? Someone new, different? Have you ever thought about what she might be wondering about? Have you ever broached the subject with her?" Aaron asked. Hearing that from someone else with a different tone I would have felt challenged, with him I didn't. I didn't answer though. He continued, "You know, 60% of husbands have erotic fantasies about their wives with other men. How about you, Brett? Are you one of the 60%? Forgive me for being intrusive, but when I meet new friends and the conversation is right, I like to conduct my informal survey. So far 60% of the men I know confirm the statistic."

"You know, that might be over the line, Aaron, as in none of your business."

Aaron laughed, "OK sorry, no offense intended, but that response was an answer in itself, don't you think?"

I did not answer the question. I was staring at my wife on the floor obviously giddy from the attention of the young man with whom she was dancing for the second time. I watched another man, closer to our age, stocky, broad shouldered, resembling a young Tom Selleck with a similar moustache, cut in. Before she started to dance with her new partner, she grabbed the young man's hand, taking his pen from his shirt pocket, and wrote on his hand, glancing at me and giving him what I recognized as her teasing laughing. Eleanor twirled away from him and into the Selleck lookalike's arms, who was a bit surer of himself, not pulling her close at first, but gradually becoming bolder, his hand running up and down her back, as if heading for her ass sooner or later.

"It's OK to admit it," Aaron said, also watching Eleanor. "I understand completely. In my line of work, I tend to study people, habits, common traits, things about themselves they think they are concealing but they are not." He looked up. "Am I wrong? Is it not exciting to see your wife wanted by her dance partners, to see how she is pressing against them, responding, feeling it, teasing, yielding to the attention? You know her mind is wondering, don't you? It is hot, absolutely. Actually, it is closer to normal than you think to feel that way instead of immature jealously."

It crossed my mind that Aaron had not been invited to analyze what I was thinking, or what my wife was thinking, even if he was right, but he had pegged exactly what had been running through my mind as I watched my wife dance.

"If you've not thought about that aspect of what your wife might want, what she might fantasize about, as empty nesters it might be something to think about. Just a suggestion, don' t mean to pry," Aaron said, "But you two are nice people, sometimes I intrude places I should not, just force of habit with my job. Please forgive me if I have gotten too personal."

24

Eleanor had taken a couple of glasses of wine from the waiters' trays as they passed through the crowd on the dance floor, and her glassy look told me she had a great buzz going, when she stumbled, her partner caught her, pulling her too him again, his left hand sliding to her breast and copping a quick feel that was far outside merely catching her.

Eleanor did not push him away, but I was unsure if she was too drunk to realize what was happening. I started to get up and break it up, this was getting over the line when Aaron stopped me with a, "Permit me, less obtrusive to the room," he said. "Another man cutting in versus a pissed off husband. No need to create a scene unnecessarily."

"OK," I said, sitting down, watching as Aaron cut in, obviously to the displeasure of the stocky mustached man, but he relinquished his hold on my wife and Eleanor wrapped her arms around Aaron's neck, rescued. They finished the dance, danced another two before he guided her back to the table.

"I need some water," she said.

"I'll get it," I said, stepping back to the bar. There was a long line and it took a while. I saw her and Aaron lean toward each other in their continued private conversation.

Eleanor was bobbing her head, she was more drunk than I realized, and I knew it was time to get her back to the room and said so.

"Yes, a good time to call it a night," Aaron said. "I've enjoyed the company of you two, why don't we get together sometimes when I am working up your way, say a nice dinner, my treat," he said.

"That would be nice," Eleanor said. I nodded my head, reaching in my wallet for a business card, and he gave me one of his. Old school. Not putting it in his phone first.

"Thanks for rescuing me," Eleanor said, pulling Aaron close for a quick kiss on the lips, over done some due to her inebriation, lasting longer than a normal kiss. She broke away.

"Delightful meeting both of you," Aaron said, and he was gone.

Eleanor was on both a high from the booze, and a high from the attention. In our car back to the motel she was babbling on about her excitement. "Damn, did you see how that young guy was all over me," she laughed. "He wanted me so bad, and I'm old enough to be his mother."

"Really?" I said, acting as if I had not noticed.

"His big cock was grinding against me, he was rock hard, and big," she giggled. "He asked me out on a date."

"What did you say?" I asked.

"I told him I was married, and I did not date, sorry." Again, a soft giggle, "But asked me to give him my phone number so he could text me sometime, just in case I might change my mind."

"Did you?" I asked, realizing now what she had been writing on his hand.

"Change my mind, no. I was teasing. Yeah, I'll ignore him if he calls, I just thought I was a daring thing to do," she said. "I did tell him that if I wasn't married that it would be on." Eleanor giggled. "What a night, I gave my number to two different men."

26

"Two?"

"Yeah, Aaron asked for it, and I told him. I asked him if I should write it down, he asked me to say it, I did, and said, "I've got it up here," and he tapped his temple. You believe he could remember a phone number that easy?"

Chapter 3

Aaron's question about what was going through Eleanor's mind at the reception stuck in my mind on the four-hour drive home the following day. Eleanor was nursing a hangover and didn't talk a lot the first hour, but eventually the painkillers and the coffee kicked in and she eased closer to normal.

"Are you happy?" I asked.

"What kind of crazy question is that?" Eleanor asked.

"Answering a question with a question."

"Of course, I am happy. Why would you even ask that?"

"I don't know, it's, well, last night. When you were dancing with that young man."

"Eric," she interrupted.

"When you were dancing with Eric, you were so, animated, excited, enjoying the attention."

"Yes, I did enjoy it, it was exciting. It is exiting to get attention, compliments, all that," she said.

"I try to compliment you all the time. You know how hot I think you are."

"Yeah, but you're my husband, that doesn't really count, does it?"

"It is more exciting if someone else compliments you?" I asked.

"Always," Eleanor said, smiling.

"So you were excited last night, I didn't misread that."

"Oh baby, I was very excited last night." She paused. "Does that bother you?"

I thought before I answered, confronting a truth that had been lurking in the back of my mind until now. "Actually, exactly the opposite. It was hot watching you fawned over, because I knew in the end, no matter how hot you got them, I was the one taking you home."

"True," Eleanor said.

"We've never talked about this before, but was that the most excited you've been around another man? I mean it appeared there was a vibe going back and forth. I mean, I know you've been hit on as pretty as you are, a lot when I'm not around, but..."

"What are you asking?" Eleanor said.

"I am not sure exactly," I said. "I guess I'm asking about other times men have turned you on, when you've thought about other men that way."

"What way?"

"Are you telling me that you weren't thinking sexual attraction things?" I asked. "Or do you only call it flirting."

Eleanor laughed. "Flirting? I've always flirted, I like turning men on, teasing. You know that. It's fun when they respond." She smiled. "I know our sex last night in the room was great. I wasn't the only one turned on. Did my teasing those other men excite you? I always thought my flirting was something you tolerated."

"It was different the way you were flirting last night," I said. "I didn't realize your flirting with other men was hot until last night," I said, "at least that I

29

would admit it to you. I don't know how to say it last night, but my mind was playing games with me, it seemed like there was a sexual tension, like something beyond flirting was in the air." I got off the topic as I knew I was not explaining it well. "So was dancing with Eric the most you've been turned on to another man?"

"No," she said flatly. "You didn't even see it did you?"

"What do you mean?"

"I was turned on dancing with Eric, but the most I've ever been turned on was with Aaron. God he was so hot. I mean if I wasn't married, I just wanted to tell him, 'take me.' My panties were soaked when I when to the bathroom the second time, I had to wrap them in a paper towel and put them in my purse."

"You were dancing after that without panties?" I asked.

"Yeah, and you didn't notice, did you?"

"No. That's hot," I said.

"Yes, it is," she giggled. "Aaron thought so too." I jerked my head in her direction. "He noticed when he was rubbing my ass," she said.

Chapter 4

Over our years together we have not necessarily been prudes. I think we are normal in that we had our newly married phase when the thought of each other was all we needed to jump into bed at 100% horniness. Then, over the years, outside distractions crept in. Normal distractions, building a career, raising children, mortgage, car payments, braces.

When we had a chance to be alone, renew our batteries, concentrate on each other, the magic was still there, but it took more time and effort to build up to the intensity we once enjoyed. It was as if there were never enough time, we would leave each getaway seeming as if we had left something on the table.

It was on these trips Eleanor would allow herself to step a tiny bit out of her good Mom, Sunday School teacher mode. She would dress skimpier for me, showing more flesh, with my encouragement. That always turned me on, but being the modest person she is, there was always that desire within me for her to show more than she allowed.

The outside-the-box moment for us so far had been the nude beach. The effect on me when we were back in the room was as expected, a wild crazy afternoon of uninhibited sex, spurred by the fact my wife had gone completely nude on the beach, in public.

At home it doesn't work that way, despite using toys, role-playing, all the things I devised to keep our sex life exciting and new—invariably she will go along willingly, up to a point, then shut down. Her limits versus my limits are far apart, but as her husband I respect her limits, although I sometimes would prefer, she not be so conservative.

We role play other partners occasionally, more like a game though. I have fucked her while describing her fucking someone else, as elaborate and detailed as possible, and she has great orgasms from it, but at the end, every time, she cannot embrace the playing, she always puts a buzz kill at the end. "That was fun for here, but I don't want to talk about it outside the bedroom. That's not me. I'm doing this for you." I knew without saying that she knew that was one of my fantasies that I imagined happening for real, and I wished that she would at least play along with the item for a few minutes, but no.

Eleanor says that it stays fantasy, but the intensity of her orgasms is not hidden from me, although I do not confront her on how hard she cums from such themes.

Only once after a particularly intense sexual afternoon I vocalized my ultimate fantasy with her, that of watching her with someone else. "That is something that will stay a fantasy, buster," Eleanor said firmly.

"I wasn't saying you should, only that it a fantasy, like winning the lottery or something like that is a fantasy."

"I'll take that under advisement," Eleanor said, and the subject did not come up again. She didn't voice her fantasy despite my asking, but from gauging her reactions when we played our games, I had a good guess. For sure I know what turned her on, fantasy or no.

***

The difference on the drive back from the wedding was that for that night rather than just talking about teasing and flirting, she had openly been overtly sexual in front of me, not just flirting but touching. She had danced close enough to feel the distant heat of the flame before darting back out of reach. This was a step outside her comfort zone. A second step was admitting how attracted she had been to Aaron.

I thought after the weeding encounter we had heard the last of Aaron and the young man, Eric. Back home we fell quickly into our work, home, dinner, TV till bedtime routine, interspaced one or two nights a week with a foray to the hot tub with drinks, followed by slow casual comfortable sex.

Yes, I thought I had heard the last of them, but I was wrong.

Chapter 5

Four weeks later I received an unexpected call, it was from Aaron. "Hi Brett, this is Aaron Davidson, from the wedding. How are you?"

"I'm good, Aaron, and yourself?"

"Fine, I wanted to call, as I am going to be at a business meeting in a resort about 30 minutes from you. I was wondering if I could buy dinner for you and your lovely wife?"

"I'm not sure," I said. "If we don't have a conflict that would be fine."

"Do you have a conflict?" Aaron asked.

"Let me check," I said, opening my calendar. "Friday or Saturday?" I asked.

"Friday is good," Aaron said.

"Let me call Eleanor and see with her…"

"Brett, if I may ask a favor, let me call and ask her. Let's try something she is not expecting." He was confident that was for sure, and smooth. In a single sentence he was asking my permission to call my wife—and at the same time putting me in an awkward position for me to say no.

I stammered an answer, "Uh OK, uh have her call me to confirm if that what she wants to do."

"Thanks," Aaron said.

"You need the number?"

"No, I have it," he said.

***

I waited 30 minutes with no call from Eleanor, got interrupted with a small work fire I had to put out, got everything rolling smooth again, and glanced at my phone. It was an hour and 10 minutes. I dialed her number and got the recording. She was still on the phone.

The phone rang an hour and 55 minutes after I had hung up from Aaron. Eleanor sounded bubbly. "Hey baby, I just got off the phone with Aaron, it looks like we are getting a free dinner Friday night."

"You didn't have a conflict? I thought you had a bridal shower to go to or something."

Eleanor laughed, "I don't now," she said. "I'm sending a gift to them instead."

"Have you been on the phone with Aaron all this time?" I asked.

"Yes."

"What on earth did you talk about?"

"A little bit of everything, lot of nothing. He tells such fascinating stories. He's been everywhere and done everything I think, so interesting to talk to. Sorry I talked that long, but it didn't seem that long when we were talking. It was like talking to an old friend, and I cannot explain that feeling."

"Not a problem," I said, because I had nothing that I could say after that. What would I say? She seemed to have an innocent answer for everything.

"I'm leaving work a little early, I'm going shopping for a new dress," Eleanor said, "And I have to schedule a pedi and mani."

***

Friday night I arrived home late, and Eleanor was in a tizzy. My suit was on the bed with a shirt. "I'm commandeering our bath; I'm running late getting ready. You need to get ready in the guest bath. I'm hurrying as fast as I can." Eleanor was leaned over the sink, a hair dryer in her left hand, a towel wrapped around her body.

My Dopp kit for traveling was in the closet, so getting ready in the guest bath was not a problem. I showered, shaved, poured myself a glass of wine and sat in my easy chair waiting on my wife. It was time to leave to be there on time, but still no movement from the bedroom.

I heard her heels on the hardwood floor before I saw her, and I gasped as she glided down the stairs. Her dark hair was shining in the light, flowing down on her shoulders in soft waves framing her model face, dark smoky eyes that made her green eyes stand out, the brightest red lipstick I had ever seen her wear, and she was in a white tank dress, very tight showing off her gym body, dropping almost to her ankles, but with a low scooped back and deep U-shaped front displaying a lot of cleavage. The top resembled a white one-piece swimsuit, but longer with a skirt bottom.

Despite my encouragement over the years, a dress this revealing was something she would only wear on vacation far away from home, and it would take a day of urging and three glasses of wine for her to go out dressed this hot. This was the most daring and revealing clothing I had ever seen her wear, even on vacations.

She was wearing large hoop earrings, and a pendant on a long chain that rested between her breasts. Her heels completed the outfit.

"Wow, you are breath taking," I said. "New dress. Sexy plus, I love how you are showing off the goods for a change."

"Yes, a new special occasion dress. Glad you like it." she said.

I had to ask. "Wearing this just for Aaron?" I said.

"No, I'm wearing it for you, you are always pushing for me to be sexier. I saw this in the window at the mall and it was an impulse thing. It is an impulse thing to wear this out in public, but I knew you would like it, you know, all part of this empty nest adjusting. For you baby. It's a little flirtier, don't you think? You say you like me flirtier."

I raised my near empty wine glass. "Here's to impulses."

"We'll see how much my dressing hotter and flirting turn you on when we get home."

"You are going to get flirtier with Aaron that you were at the wedding?" I asked.

"You said you liked it, so perhaps, we'll see," she smiled, saying nothing more.

***

Eleanor made an entrance when we entered the small upscale restaurant adjoining the resort. I heard a couple of conversations stop among those waiting for seating. Aaron was waiting in the foyer, standing when Eleanor came into the door greeting her with a with a warm smile, staring at her for a few seconds before reaching for her in a quick hug. He gave her a buss on the cheek.

"Unbelievable," Aaron said. "You are stunning tonight, Eleanor."

"Thank you, kind sir," she said, moving closer to him, taking his arm at the elbow as the hostess led up to the table toward the back of the room.

"I prefer corner tables," Aaron explained, "they are quieter."

There was something about Aaron that caused us open up with him, his manner of asking questions and listening carefully to our answers, talking about our interests, favorite places, things he asked I do not recall anyone asking before. As we talked and answered his questions, I noticed he paid close attention, not interrupting, a good listener, and interjecting an appropriate story at just the right time. I had to admit I was enjoying Aaron's company. We shared common thoughts about politics, sports, and life in general. He established a connection. He was fast becoming a friend.

The dinner was perfect, steaks with marinated mushrooms and onions, an Italian chopped salad, and potatoes au gratin. I was not familiar with the wine, but it was smooth, went down easy, and we were halfway through the second bottle when the lights dimmed and a sliding wall opened, revealing a dance floor, and a small band playing smooth on the stage.

Aaron was smiling. "This was an old dance hall in the 40's. I hope you enjoy the surprise," Aaron said. "This band is highly recommended, and I remember how much I enjoyed dancing with Eleanor the last time we were together. I hope you do not mind my being so presumptuous," Aaron said.

"Not at all," I said. My wife was beaming. "Dance away."

Eleanor gave me a warm smile and took Aaron's extended hand and they danced three songs, talking during the entire time, and I watched my wife's face, animated, smiling, flipping her hair, shaking her head, tossing it back. Aaron remained the gentleman, his hand on her bare back, his other holding her palm in a classic dancing position, but their bodies were touching lightly. At the end of the third song, they returned to the table, holding hands. I had a fresh bottle of wine on the table.

Eleanor was giddy, happy and smiling. Aaron sat down and smiled. "Thanks for letting me go first, your turn, husband. I shouldn't monopolize your wife as much as I would love too."

"Thank you," I said, waiting until the next song started and taking my wife to the dance floor. "Having a good time," I asked.

"I am having a great time, are you?" she asked. "I don't want to ignore you or make you feel like a third wheel, you might want to take more of a part in the conversation," she said. I didn't say that it was difficult with her sitting with her back to me and her head almost touching Aaron's, but I kept quiet.

39

"I love you. I love to see you enjoying yourself. When you do that you glow," I said.

"I am enjoying this," she said, "Thanks for accepting Aaron's invitation. This is fun," as the song ended. I held on to her hand as she tried to move back to the table.

"Hang on, one more," I said. The dance was a slow foxtrot and as we started the steps, her graceful, me clumsy. "How do you see this night going?" I said.

"Oh, I'm going to keep flirting and teasing Aaron, enjoy the attention and compliments he is laying on, maybe come on to him a little for your benefit, and like Cinderella at midnight I will leave the handsome dashing prince and go home with you." She paused. "You weren't inferring anything else, were you?" Her face changed. "Oh my God, you are thinking about your fantasy, are you?"

I did not want to lie, but at that moment that was exactly what I was thinking and I felt as if my wife was reading my mind. Aaron seemed like the perfect candidate, and this could easily be the right place and right time. I said nothing. "I've told you, that stays a fantasy," Eleanor said. "This is all just fun, nothing more."

"I said nothing in that vein, you can't condemn me for my thoughts," I teased. "You are going home with me."

I'm not sure if it was the wine, the giddiness, Aaron's lavish compliments, or as I said, the right time and the right place but I was shocked at what my wife said next. "I'm going home with you, but I take it that I have your permission to get bolder, a little flirtier and more suggestive, push the boundaries a little."

"Whatever you would like," I said.

"Well baby, you just wait, I am going to have some fun with all this tonight," Eleanor said, "Some for you, but I'm not going to lie; I'm going to enjoy the hell out of this too."

The song ended and we returned to the table, Eleanor downed another glass of wine and stood facing Aaron. "Come on boyfriend, let's dance the night away."

I'm not sure if it was the wine, or my wife trying to let go, or wanting to put on a show, but what followed was a sultry, sensuous dance that seemed as if she and Aaron had melded their bodies together. Her head tossing was more animated, her laugh more relaxed but excited, her alluring come-take-me smile telling me more than words as I watched her dance, flirt, and tease her dance partner.

They dance in my sight but in the darkened corner of the dance floor. Eleanor and Aaron continued dancing for almost an hour, pausing only to return to the table to refill their wine glasses from the table bottle I kept freshly ordered. They did defer to me to some extent, asking if I minded if they continued dancing, but Eleanor did not ask me to dance with her again, or give any indication that she wanted me to take a turn on the dance floor.

It was approaching closing for the night, so I ordered a final bottle for last call, and glanced back to see my wife and Aaron no longer dancing but now

41

locked in an embrace, kissing, a passionate embrace, swaying to the music. I was transfixed.

This was my modest wife kissing another man openly, eagerly, as if he was a lover, there in front of me. "I'm doing this for you," I kept hearing in my head, watching as Aaron's hands slid down to cup her ass and pull her hard against him, a move that told me he was grinding his erection against her belly, as no man could be in his place and not be rock hard.

I don't know how long they kissed, but they eventually broke and laughing returned to the table for refills, with Aaron's arm around her waist. Eleanor thanked me for ordering another bottle, finishing the glasses quickly and putting the empty glasses on the table.

Returning to the corner for the next few minutes they started kissing more than dancing again, although making little attempt to sway with the music, picking up where they left off with kissing. Eleanor broke the kiss and resumed the slower dance step, not in rhythm to the music but slower, whispering, smiling, smiling at me with a slight nod as she locked eyes with me over Aaron's shoulder. After a few turns they kissed again, making out like horny teenagers.

Aaron took more liberties, whispering in her ear as his hands slid down her side to her hip, easing around to her ass but she grabbed his wrist and lifted his hand to her breast, the strap sliding off her shoulder. He deftly turned that side of her to the wall and eased her top down, baring her breast but quickly covering it with his hand, discreetly, no one in the

42

room noticing, but me. I was too stunned to move. I could not believe this was happening and had no clue how I should react.

When they broke the kiss again, Aaron continued to cup her bare breast until she deftly pulled the strap back up, just in time, as the lights came up and the sound system announced, "Closing in five minutes."

Eleanor was panting as she approached the table, a thin sheen of sweat on her upper chest, her red lipstick worn away. Aaron did not seem embarrassed that he had been kissing and feeling up my wife in front of me, instead with a confident air extended his hand, ending the evening without protest. "Thank you so much for joining me for dinner and allowing me the pleasure of dancing with the lovely Eleanor, Brett," he said. "Are you two sure you are able to drive home?" he asked.

"I think so," I said. Eleanor poured the last of the bottle into her glass and Aaron's. He noticed me weave when I stood.

"Naah," Aaron said. "I'm springing for an Uber."

"Our car," I protested.

"Join me to watch football tomorrow in the bar here. I'll spring for the Uber back, and you can pick up your car then, safely and sober."

I didn't argue. I knew I was too drunk to drive. "Sounds like a plan," I said, recognizing the wisdom of that.

Eleanor moved to steady me. "Take good care of my friend," Aaron said to Eleanor, following us out the front to the waiting Uber. I climbed into the back seat, scooted over to allow Eleanor in from the street

43

side, and watched as Eleanor turned and gave Aaron a kiss, not a buss but another long embracing kiss like she had on the dance floor.

"I had a spectacular time tonight," she said.

"I'm glad you did. We must do it again next time I'm up this way."

"Let's" Eleanor said.

In the car my wife snuggled under my arm, and the Uber driver offered no conversation, clearly not understanding what he had witnessed, a beautiful woman in the lowcut sexy white dress locking lips with one man and crawling into the cab and sliding under the arm of another.

Eleanor kissed me as passionately as she had Aaron as we pulled out of the resort and whispered. "Did you enjoy the show?"

"Yes."

"Aaron said you would like it. I enjoyed it to. It was hot, kissing him, knowing you were watching, my body telling me to do more, my mind telling me no, but I knew this ended at midnight and it did."

"Yes it did. You are going home with me."

"And when I get you home, I am going to wear you out tonight," she said. "No need for foreplay, I've already done all that here. My pussy is soaked."

***

In the bedroom I fervently peeled her out of the white dress almost in ritual movements, the straps down her shoulders, her bare breasts popping free, no bra to deal with, down over her hips, surprised to

44

discover no panties. She had been without any form of underwear all night. I touched her pussy, she was dripping.

I kissed her hard, with a genuine hunger. I could smell his cologne on her, feeling the press of her body against me, as another man had enjoyed tonight, and then I enjoyed what Aaron did not, the pleasure of opening her legs, moving between them and plunging my hard cock inside her moist pussy.

Eleanor was alive, a tigress, a bucking bronc, meeting my thrusts with urgent demanding thrusts of her own, our bodies slamming together, popping flesh, cumming quickly and never stopping, a quick hard urgent fuck.

I plunged into her moist pussy hard, fired on knowing another man had been in her head tonight, wondered if she was imagining him fucking her, and determined to fuck those thoughts out of my wife's head. She came again, at the exact moment I was spewing my come inside her waiting pussy.

I rolled off her, retrieved a warm wet washcloth from the bathroom, handed it to her and she wiped at the cum I had deposited, scooting over under my arm.

"Damn that was good. I should tease men more often," she said.

"Pretty good results."

"So what did you think?" Eleanor asked.

"What do you mean?"

"Seeing me kissing Aaron the way we did? What did you think when you saw him touching my ass, or when he slid the strap off my shoulder, and I let him caress my bare boob?"

"I saw it. It was hot. It was clear that you were turned on, else you would not have done it," I said. "You seemed to be enjoying it so much I didn't feel right to stop you."

"I was," she said, "But me stepping out of my comfort zone was for you too," my wife said. "What were you thinking though," Eleanor persisted. "Were you jealous, angry, wanting to get up and barge between us, what?"

I thought about my answer before speaking. "I thought it was erotic," I said. "I was rock hard watching you. I wasn't angry, or jealous, surprisingly. Okay, I have never been so turned on." I paused. "And I was curious."

"Curious?" she asked. "About what?"

"About how far you would take it, how far would you let him go? How far you wanted him to go," I said. "I've never seen you be so forward."

"Did you get your answer?"

"Not exactly," I said. "I saw how far you went. I don't know how far you wanted to go."

"This was all over the line, I know. I am sorry if it bothers you." Eleanor said, "But I stopped where I wanted, I did not dare go further. What I wanted has nothing to do with it."

"Well, it was the hottest thing I have ever seen you do," I said. "It didn't bother me. I had to sit most of the time to conceal my erection."

Eleanor gave a soft laugh, "He was right."

"What?"

"Aaron said this would be your reaction."

"Really?"

46

"Yes. And he said you would want me to go further when you thought about it more. I did tell him that my having sex with someone else was one of your fantasies."

"He's being a little presumptuous, he doesn't know what I think. I may straighten him out about that a lunch tomorrow," I said. "Are you coming?"

"No, you guys can do this football thing all on your own, I suspect I'm going to be hungover and will need to sleep till noon."

Chapter 6

I was in the bar at the resort at 11:30, Aaron was seated at a table toward the back, facing the wall size tv. He shook my hand, waved for the bartender and bartender sat a Weller and water bourbon in front of me.

"I took the liberty of checking out their bourbon list, I saw you were drinking Buffalo Trace last night, I figured you would be good for 12year- old-Weller."

"Perfect, thank you," I said, taking a sip of the expensive bourbon.

"I want to thank you for last night, it was a most enjoyable evening. It is nice to find friends to visit when I am required to stay away from home," Aaron said. "I hope you enjoyed it too."

"Thank you, I know it was an expensive meal last night."

"Worth every penny," he smiled. "Business expense as far as the IRS is concerned, you are potential clients, if anyone should ask. And how is Eleanor this morning?"

"Hungover," I said. "She said she had a good time last night and said to tell you thanks."

"Eleanor is a vivacious, delightful woman, I thank you for sharing her with me," he said. "That is one of the reasons I asked you here today."

"Why is that?" I asked.

"In my line of work, I have learned to sense things about people, reading between the lines of what they say and do, observing."

"What does that have to do with us?"

Aaron didn't answer immediately, taking a long breath. "Have you thought any more about what I asked you at the wedding?"

"What? If I ever wondered what Eleanor was thinking when she was dancing with Eric?" I asked.

"Yes, that, and wondering what was really inside her head, the part she doesn't admit to you."

"I have thought about it actually, I've tried to talk to her about fantasies, and, well it is tough for her to talk about, it always has been so with her," I said.

"I know," Aaron said. "She told me."

"When did she tell you that?" I asked, probing.

Aaron smiled a confident smile, "Eleanor gave me her number at the wedding, we've texted a few times, shared a few emails. She didn't want to talk on the phone until you were in the loop, but we touched on some of the things you and I have been talking about."

"You've been carrying on some correspondence with my wife behind my back?" I said it brusque and louder.

"I wouldn't put it like that," Aaron said. "I would say more like two friends talking. I did ask her to save the texts and emails so you would not be upset when we got around to having this conversation."

"This conversation?" I asked.

"Yes," Aaron said. "I anticipated you and I having this conversation, I have asked her to save all the texts for your review after our talk. I assure you I am a friend. I'm trying to help. Please don't take it the wrong way."

"In what way?" I said.

"In the life counseling side of my work I seek to help people, to find win-win-win situations. Part of my motivational business is personal counseling along those lines, helping people maximize their potential, enjoy themselves with confidence as they do. I have achieved a high percentage of success."

"OK."

"I charge large sums for my services typically, but not for friends. As I said the other evening, I am trying to spend more time smelling the roses, give a little back to a world that has blessed me with success. I'm offering a short version of my personal life enhancement course to you and Eleanor."

"I don't think we have extra money to spend on something…"

"I am not asking for money, I would not charge you anything," Aaron said.

"What's the catch?" I asked.

"No catch," Aaron said, "I like to do nice things for nice people. I guess you could say I'm trying to bank some good karma. You two qualify. I think you two could benefit greatly from this course. You are empty nesting, a time of readjusting and often confusion, and my course gives you both a solid baseline."

"And what does this course entail?" I asked.

"On your part consulting with me, some online, some chats on the phone, more so after the course than during. Eleanor, well, that would require in person sessions."

The red flags started popping up. It was starting to become clearer. "Let me sum up what I am hearing," I said. "You are trying to work this around so that you can seduce my wife?"

Aaron smiled. "Let me answer you in this way. You have told Eleanor you have a fantasy of her fucking someone else, is that right?"

"How do you know that?" I stammered.

"Aaron went immediately into a second question. "You became very turned on watching her flirt with Eric and I at the wedding, and your wife and I kissing at dinner last night, didn't you?"

I said nothing but there was no pause to interject anything.

"You were shocked but turned on when you saw me touching Eleanor's breast. I bet it excited you to realize she was allowing me to touch her intimately. You know how soft and lovely touching her breast feels, you have asked her to be bolder for a long time, and however reluctant she has been in the past, this time she was. The evening was as good for you as going to a nude beach, was it not?"

I jerked my head up. How did he know that? What all had my wife been telling him?

"So, the big question is, are your willing to allow some of your fantasies come to fruition? Would you like Eleanor more sensuous, less modest, with more confidence, a woman who could boldly strip off her clothes and stroll down a nude beach with you, with hesitation or inhibition? Do you have the courage to

51

allow her to become the woman you dream of her being? Is the idea of her more confident and sensual the most erotic thing you can imagine?" Aaron paused to take a long drink of his beer before continuing, his eyes studying my face for my reaction. I felt as if he was reading me like a book. I've never been a good poker player.

"You have tried for almost 20 years to effect that change in your wife into the woman you want her to be more like. You've made some progress, but you know she is not going to allow you to do that, it is as if she is yielding too much of the husband/wife dynamic to you. Eleanor loves the balance she has with you. So the question is will you allow someone else to help Eleanor becomes the woman you would like for her to be?"

"I don't know," I said.

"Honest response," Aaron said with a soft laugh. "I'm sorry I'm dumping a lot on you, but while you and I have met twice, I've talked with Eleanor quite a bit. Frankly, if you ever want to see your wife open up, now is the time. If you want your life with her to continue exactly as it has, with her modesty, lack of confidence, I can say there is nothing wrong with that at all. You two have a good loving marriage. You must answer the question yourself; do you want more?"

"I'm not sure I know enough to answer you," I said. "Like what goes on…"

"My program works, I will not give out the details. The only thing in the end is the results that you want," Aaron said.

"That would be nice but…"

"Trust. And you must trust me and trust her or there is no need to start. At the end of the program, in only a few weeks, you get what you say you have wanted. If you have been lying to yourself, you must face that too. Do not consider anything I am saying pressure to accept my offer."

"If I said yes," I said, "Hypothetically, what can you tell me, what is required."

"First, your permission to go ahead. Second, your wife's presence for sessions on Saturdays for four weeks. I recently purchased a fully furnished cabin about a half-hour from here we are closing tomorrow, in fact.

"You would drop off Eleanor on Saturday morning at 8 a.m. for a day-long session, you pick her up at 6 p.m. for a total of four Saturdays. The next three Saturdays following, you drop her off at noon, pick her up at 1 a.m. The final Saturday, the eighth one, will be a graduation of sorts, you will bring her at noon and join us that afternoon, ending time undetermined."

I do not know why, but he was pulling me in, I could feel it. "And would this involve sex?"

"Absolutely," Aaron said. "That is the area we are targeting is it not? Everything about your life otherwise is positive, this should not affect the other aspects of your life in any way, but dramatically enhance the sexual side of your marriage, if you are truthful about wanting Eleanor less inhibited, less modest, and with more confidence in her own sexuality. You must be willing to let her be open to

53

possibilities. You have said you wanted her to experience another man, that will be a necessary part of opening the sensual side your wife has been repressing. For her to be free you must free her to explore." He paused for effect. "You must answer the question yourself, can you now let her do as you have asked of her for years?"

"And if we start and don't like it?" I said.

Aaron sensed me caving. "Eleanor says stop, all she has to do is say so, everything stops, I bring her home to you within minutes, and you two will never see me again."

"And if I say stop?"

"Please understand this is much more about her than you, and stopping in the middle of the program could possibly do more harm than good, not to mention a waste of my time and effort. I have dealt with balky husbands before men who say talk a good game but balk when it comes down to backing up their words. We are working to achieve what you want, so a part of the contract is I will not charge for the program, but you guarantee you are good for eight weeks of the program. After that, you can stop everything without penalty," Aaron said. "So there is a $10,000 penalty for your failure to allow the eight sessions. Frankly I've never had that happen."

"I need to talk to Eleanor," I said.

Aaron pointed to an old British style phone booth in the corner of the bar. "Call her, they have it soundproofed so you can hear even when the bar is noisy, you cell will work in there."

"I was thinking when I get…"

"You might be interested to know that Eleanor has already agreed, if you are willing. She wants to gain confidence herself."

"When did she…"

"Booth is right over there, do not take my word for anything. Call her," Aaron said.

I went to the booth and closed the door, blocking out the sound of the bar. Eleanor answered on the first ring. "Hey," she said. "I wondered when you would call."

"Do you know what Aaron is proposing?"

"Yes. He and I have talked back and forth about it quite a bit, emailing and texting."

"And?"

"Don't freak, and I know this sounds crazy, but I would like to do it. No, I want to do it. Not to become only the woman you want me to be, but for myself, to help me open myself up, to feel freer," my wife said.

"You think you need a course like this for that?"

"Yes, I do," she said. "And you want me to, I think. The dancing with Aaron last night, even letting him feel me up while you watched, it was a sort of test. You enjoyed what you saw, and you were thinking beyond that too, I know you. You were insatiable when we got home. I was crazy hot too. We both fed off each other and it was fantastic." Eleanor paused. "I love you, Brett," she said. "And I know you. I think that you are going to tell Aaron to proceed with the program. I am not rushing into this, I have considered it from many different angles. I want to be the woman you want me to be and I think

55

this course will help be that person. If you do say yes, I'll start next Saturday. I'm in if you are."

"And if I say no?" I asked.

"No means no. You are my husband, and I will not go against you, but if you say no, never bring up the other man fantasy again, not talking, not role-playing, never. Understand? No longer tease my mind."

"I need to think," I said, ending the call, walking outside rather than back to Aaron's table. Here it was, facing reality or keep it forever my fantasy only a fantasy. I knew within me that if I balked on this, our roles were basically set for the future. I had talked a good game; was it only talk? I sat on the bench gazing out at the mountain view for five minutes, then rose, my mind made up. I went to Aaron's table.

"I'm in," I said.

"Are you sure?" he asked.

"Yes."

"OK, I only need your signature on one piece of paper," he said, reaching inside his pocket and unfolding a white sheet, extending a pen. I read it, and it was simple and succinct, if I withdrew from the 8-week program anytime during those eight weeks, I would pay a 10,000-dollar exit fee. Eleanor could say no and end it at any time. I signed the paper.

We watched a couple of football games, neither team a favorite, drank two pitchers of beer, and talked about a variety of things, everything except the fact I would be delivering my wife to him for a day, without knowing exactly what would happen, but a strong conviction that when I picked her up on

56

Saturday, my fantasy of her fucking someone else will likely be fulfilled.

Chapter 7

Eleanor was apprehensive when I came home. "Hey baby," she said. "How was your afternoon?"

"I guess we need to talk," I said. "You are totally on board with all this?"

"Yes," she said. "You signed. Aaron texted me."

"You didn't hesitate in answering," I said.

"I've thought it through, talked it through long before today, and I believe at this point in our lives this is the best thing I can do right now."

"And that is?"

"Trying to be the woman you want me to be. I understand you want this for me, not to control me, but to free me," Eleanor said. "I think you were too close to me to explain it in a manner I could understand it. Talking with Aaron makes it much clearer. He helped me figure it all out. And while I say in ways, I am doing this for you, I am also doing it for myself too. A win-win."

"And do you know what you can expect on Saturday?" I asked.

Eleanor still gave me her shy reserved smile. "Aaron has been vague, he said we'd start out with some frank and honest conversation, about my goals, you, me, and he says depending on my answers will guide the direction of where the program needs to go. He gave me a map to his cabin, if you can call it that. Actually, it is a large house with a magnificent view." She studied my face. "This is what you said you wanted. Are you having second thoughts?"

"No, I signed the paper, I agreed. I'm more worried about you."

"Why would you be worried?" Eleanor asked, with a knowing smile. "I can stop anytime by saying no and everything ends at that moment. I trust him in that. You must trust me that if anything gets out of line, I'll walk out."

It was time to confront the beast. "Aaron wants to fuck you."

"Yes, and you have said you wanted me to fuck someone else, and I think the role playing has influenced me, and now your fantasy is mine too. I want to fuck someone else. No, that's not right, I want to fuck Aaron. He has seduced me, although it was not a hard thing to do, and unless you have changed our mind about your desires for me, it is what I plan to do, probably Saturday."

Hearing my wife say that, I gave an audible gasp. She stopped for a second, the reality sinking in.

"I think in the long run this program Aaron is talking about will be good for both of us—but I promise you I am not doing anything you do not want to happen. If you want to end all this right now, say so. I won't go Saturday; I'll call Aaron and call the whole thing off. No harm, no foul. We have a good life the way we are," Eleanor said.

I had my finger on the kill switch in my mind. All I had to do was balk. What I had fantasized about for years, what I had imagined and cajoled my wife about—I could say I was wrong and stop right here. All I had to do was tell my wife to say no and she would. But I couldn't say it. Not knowing exactly what would happen was a concern, but knowing what was probably going to happen, my mind in turmoil it became clear.

My mind roiled, I felt queasy but I managed, "I don't want it to affect us," I said.

"I don't either, except make our life together better. I think it will."

"Then have a good time Saturday, I trust you to do whatever you think you should," I said.

"Even if included allowing another man to enjoy my body? To put his hard penis inside me?" she asked.

"Even that," I said.

"Good," Eleanor smiled. "No need to worry about it then. Get yourself a drink and I'll start supper."

After supper it was wine by the pool, and as if a signal came on about dark, we were going upstairs two hours before bedtime to make love with a newlywed urgency. The thought of what was coming was stimulating both of us to a level I would never had dreamed—including my quick recovery time. I got my wife off four times that night using my fingers, mouth, and cock. I came twice, exhausted we both went to sleep.

The rest of the week sex was in the forefront of everything. We only skipped one night because I was required to work over because of an office crisis. If anything each fuck was more intense each night, building, and then all to soon it was Friday, and the next morning I would deliver my wife for the first day of Aaron's program, deliver her to the man she had stated she was planned on fucking.

Chapter 8

Saturday morning Eleanor was up early, showered, and I noted wearing new sexy red lace bra and panties, over which she pulled a mundane red skirt with a white blouse and flat shoes, the kind of thing she might wear to work on any given day. She didn't act nervous, more like anticipating. She was excited, and I mentioned it. I can read her sometimes. She was trying to hold back and not let me see how excited she was.

"Baby, this is exciting, what else could it be, departing on a new adventure," Eleanor smiled. "I love you," she said, pulling me tight and kissing me. "This is going to be great for us, wait and see."

I hoped I was as convinced as she was, but I still felt overwhelmed. She didn't say more as I followed the directions on the GPS, winding through the hills until we came to a long driveway. We climbed to a large house on the side of the hill, a large deck overlooking an impressive mountain view. I looked around and could see no other house in view. The car clock said it was 40 minutes from home. I stopped in the drive, my heart thumping. "Well I guess this is it," I said.

"It is," Eleanor smiled. "I'm supposed to go to the door, he's not coming out to walk me in," she said. I looked up and Aaron appeared in the doorway for a second, then disappeared, the door remaining open. She took a deep breath. "OK, here I go. See you at six." She gave me a kiss, got out and stepped to the door, entering, and closing the door behind her.

I drove home with second thoughts and nervousness closing in, feeling empty—and alone. I tried to make it a usual Saturday. It didn't work. I was fidgety, I couldn't concentrate. I checked my email. There was one from Aaron. I opened it. The time stamp indicated it had been sent while I had been driving Eleanor to him.

"Hi Brett, I know this is a tough day for you, but I want to reassure you that Eleanor participating in this program will change both your lives in the most positive ways. She texted this morning that you were leaving to deliver her to me, so I assume that neither of you had cold feet to the point of calling it off, so I wanted to send this reassuring email for when you get home and are waiting until pick-up time.

I'm sure you will have a thousand questions, but an important part of this program is having time for Eleanor to process in between meetings. To that end please do not expect Eleanor to give you a detailed play by play at this point. Part of the program rules is to not discuss the process with anyone else, including spouses, and do not divulge what happens in the sessions. I ask you to respect that. Your wife will be treated well and is completely safe. That I guarantee. Our journey begins.

When you arrive this afternoon to pick Eleanor up, there is no need to come to the door, in fact I prefer you not. She will be ready to be returned to you at six.

63

Part of this program is not that she is driving herself here, it is more that symbolically you are delivering her to me, and I am returning her back to you. This is reinforcement that you are participating, and during the that time to demonstrate when she is here she will be mine.

I re-read the email twice and spent the rest of the day in a fog. I had no other alternative now. I was sitting in his drive at 5:55. At six on the dot the door opened, and Eleanor walked through, dressed only in a long tee shirt that hit her mid-thigh. Her ample breasts were alive, loose and free, bouncing wildly under the cloth as she approached. Her hair was damp, freshly showered, and she was devoid of make-up. She looked fresh and happy, smiling. She was carrying a small grocery bag bearing the clothes she had worn to him this morning.

"Hey baby," she said, with a grin, taking her seat and buckling up. I waited for her to say something, but she didn't. I started the drive home.

"Well?" I said.

"You read Aaron's email. I can't talk about it right now. Maybe after the program ends, but not now. I hope you understand," she said.

"Why?"

"Part of the program. Aaron said. I agreed. I do not understand the why," she said.

"You are going to abide by that? Keep me in the dark?"

"For the moment, yes," she said. "I'm sorry."

"What can you tell me about today?"

64

"It was good, very eye opening and introspective, I think I benefited a lot from the session."

"That it?" I said.

"Until we get home," she giggled. "This is not the place."

I practically drug her upstairs, but she was matching me step for step. In the bedroom she eagerly shucked the tee and was naked underneath. I looked over her body for tell-tale signs of sex, a bruise, a hickey, anything out of the ordinary. Nothing. She looked as beautiful and fresh as when she left that morning. We kissed and laid on the bed, our hands roaming over each other. It felt different in some way.

Eleanor broke our kiss, our bodies wrapped around each other. "OK, I can tell you now," she said. "You wanted me to fuck another man, and today I did. No details other than it was good, I enjoyed it, and now I need to enjoy you, and I want you to enjoy your wife that has realized one of your fantasies, and this time you need to be sure you reclaim your wife's pussy."

My head went in such a swirl with those words I do not remember exactly what unfurled in the minutes that followed, other than it was some of the best sex of my life, an orgasm that drained me physically and mentally. I was too weak to move. Eleanor didn't feel different physically, and had she not told me what had occurred, there was no indication that she was any different. It was as it was before—except for my knowledge for the first time in

65

20 years my wife had opened her legs and permitted another man to push his hard cock inside her—and liked it.

***

The next week our life was as normal as it had been the week before, as if nothing had happened. Eleanor had a bit more of a bounce in her step, more animated in her speech, smiling more, obviously feeling good. She would have moments in which I noticed she would be staring off, concentrating about something but I did not know what. She rebuffed my attempts to bring the previous Saturday into the equation. I didn't push it.

I heard no more from Aaron, and it didn't appear that Eleanor was texting back and forth a lot, but I respected her privacy and didn't snoop. In eight weeks when this was over, I was expecting a full detailed account, and told her so.

"Absolutely," she said.

I was on a sexual high though, the thought of my wife sharing the most intimate parts of her being with someone else was like an aphrodisiac. We made love four out of the next five nights.

I started to make a sexual advance on Friday night, but she resisted. "Not tonight please," she said. "I want to be fresh for tomorrow." That was a reality check for me. She was planning on getting fucked again tomorrow. I didn't ask her. I didn't have to.

***

All too soon, the second Saturday was here. My wife carried a shoulder bag this time, I assumed to carry her clothes she was wearing there, this time jeans and a sweatshirt, very casual. I noticed she did not wear a bra.

Again I watched her disappear into the doorway. Aaron did not appear. As she had gotten out, I noticed the zipper on her shoulder bag was partially undone, and I could see green lace and blue lace. I know she had bras in that color, and I pondered that as I drove home. I don't know why but I went to the bedroom and opened the drawer in which she keeps her bras. It was empty. No bras.

***

That afternoon when I picked up Eleanor, or as Aaron said, when he returned her to me, was a repeat of the previous Saturday. She wore the same long tee out to the car, nude underneath, her jeans and sweatshirt in the shoulder bag, her hair damp, no makeup. She was smiling, but it was a weaker smile, as if she was tired.

The urgency of the previous week was there for me, but not her. On the drive home she asked to drive through take out for supper. "I'm sorry but I'm too tired to cook. I'd like to get a nap when we get home," she said.

"No problem," I said. "Are you OK?"

"Yeah, I'm good, great even, just tired."

"And what can you tell me about this Saturday?" I asked.

"Nothing. You know that."

"Did you get fucked again?"

"I can't say," she said.

"Would you say if you didn't?" I asked.

"I can't say. I told you. Part of the program. Aaron said you wouldn't like this silence part, but he said the word to give you is 'patience.'"

"I'm not good at that," I said.

"No, you are not, but this time for this you must be. OK? Please don't push me. Please."

"Fair enough," I said.

***

That second Saturday night when I pulled her into bed after her nap and dinner, my imagination crammed with exotic possibilities to which she may have enjoyed that day, I did receive a surprise when stripped her. Her pussy was completely bare, no landing strip, nothing.

"You like it?" she asked.

"Hell yes," I said, sliding my hand over her bare pubis.

Aaron told me to do it last week, I waited until Friday. That's why I didn't want to do anything last night."

"What," I asked. "You wanted him to see your shaved pussy first?" She bowed her head and didn't answer.

68

"Well it is all yours now," she smiled. "Why don't you make use of it."

***

In the week that followed, I noticed little change from my normal wife. Eleanor remained the loving wife I had known for years. No changes in her demeanor, it was as if Saturday did not happen.

The only difference I realized is she no longer wore a bra, anytime. Shopping, dinner out, grocery store, anywhere. Her empty bra drawer remained empty, and during a blow job, for the first time she was deep throating me, engulfing my entire cock, letting it slide down her throat, her lips buried against the base of my cock. It felt great and something she had never done before, and she eagerly swallowed.

That did not mean she was flaunting her bralessness in front of me. On the contrary. No sheer tops, or extra thin blouses that kept her nipples on high beam. Still remained modest in front of me, but the gently sway of her breasts as she moved was impossible to miss.

I received an email from Aaron Sunday morning that I read before my wife woke. It read: "*I know you are somewhat anxious, and curious, but I think you should see by now that the course is not changing your day to day life with lovely Eleanor. She is indeed a prize. Your wife is excelling in her advancement through the program. She has told me her response to your questions is, as instructed, a single word. Patience. I can only reiterate that. You will find your patience amply rewarded in only a few weeks.*

The opportunity to participate in this program is a boon to your marriage at this point in your lives. You are rediscovering each other as empty nesters, and how you set the base now will affect the rest of your lives together. There is no stronger base than honesty, openness, and the ability to express it to each other. I think you know the person that needs work with not holding things back is Eleanor. You should be happy and encouraged with her progress, as you will learn at the end of the program.

Part of this program on your side is to accustom you in dealing with the unknown factor, how your mind plays all kinds of crazy games on what could be occurring with your wife when you give her to me for the day. I know it doesn't help, but, yes, there could be all kinds of crazy games. Coping with your emotions without the facts is an important part of the program for your growth. This program is for both of you.

For that brief time each Saturday that loan her to me you are both figuratively and emotionally relinquishing your marital rights to your woman, and when you free her of her marital obligations, you are not only freeing her but you are freeing yourself as well.

Chapter 9

The third Saturday came, something of a routine now, no significant change in Eleanor. I delivered her to Aaron, picked her up with her nude underneath the usual long tee with her hair damp and with the faint smell of soap. The rest of the week was a normal week, excepting her heightened libido. We fucked more than we had as newlyweds. Maybe we were feeding off each other, but something was working.

***

Monday, I received another email from Aaron, asking for my feedback, with photos attached of three models in sexy clothing, copied from clubwear websites, I assumed. His request. "Please pick which one of these you like the best." There were three different photos. The first outfit was a super short black skirt, a micro-mini, coupled with a low dipping cowl neck top, short enough to show some midriff, and an open back held together with only a couple of laces.

The second outfit was a lace dress, an open weave but closer knit around the nipples and pussy, with a bolero vest. The last was a thin tight white jersey dress, scooped arm holes with a zipper over the entire front, it zipped up from the bottom and from the top. Even zipped up it was thin enough to display the hint of a shadow of the wearer's nipples.

71

I picked the first one and hit send. Aaron responded with a "Thanks," and that was all. No explanation or why. I was still in the dark on what was occurring with my wife.

My lack of knowledge boiled over and turned into an argument later Monday afternoon. I told Eleanor I wasn't sure I could go on without knowing. She still refused to give any details, and the words escalated.

Eleanor was not screaming but she was angry, and then her voice got scary calm. "You tell me to stop, I will stop. But it will be you stopping, not me. We will take a 10 grand hit if you want to go that route. I'm not going to be the one to quit. I feel like I am making real progress, this is helping me. You signed off on this in writing. Are you changing your mind halfway through?"

I caved. She was determined to go on and I could see it. "I only want to know what is going on," I said.

"You will know in four more weeks," she said. "You can handle not knowing for four more weeks, can't you?"

"I guess," I said, "If you want me too."

"That's what I said, isn't it?"

"Yes."

"OK then," I said.

Throughout the rest of the week Eleanor reassured me that everything was OK several times, and each time she assured me that in the end I would love the result.

**

72

The fourth Saturday was the last daytime session. When I arrived on time, Eleanor did not come out of the door immediately. She was over five minutes late. I remained in the car. The door opened, and my wife came out slowly, taking small steps, a little unsteady, her smile was a very tired smile.

I knew that was fruitless to ask questions. On the drive home Eleanor dozed. I helped her upstairs and instead of what was usually a raucous sexual romp, today she asked me to let her nap.

I helped her off with her long tee and on with a flannel gown, noticing small bruises on her breasts and inner thighs for the first time. Her nipples seemed puffy, larger, like I had never seen them. She saw me staring and looked up at me with a weak, "I did have a good time. Aaron says I am progressing well and to tell you that you should be pleased." She lay down and pulled the bedspread over her as I closed the curtains. I think she was asleep before I left the room. Eleanor slept and did no stir until the next morning. I missed sex with her that night.

I had lunch ready, soup and a sandwich, when she hobbled into the kitchen. She looked tired, bags under her bloodshot eyes, her hair barely brushed. I handed her a cup of coffee and she said "Thanks."

It was time to say something. "I saw the bruises," I said.

"What?"

"You have bruises on your breasts, and on the inside of your thighs, your pussy looked rubbed almost raw. I saw when I helped you undress for bed last night," I said.

"Oh," was her only answer.

"I know you are not supposed to say anything, but I will. Are you all right? Are you being hurt? Do you need to walk away from this, like now? To Hell with the money. I mean it."

"No, no, I'm fine, I promise," Eleanor said. "We just got, I mean I didn't know I was getting a bruise at the time. I'm good. I'm sorry if that upsets you. If I thought I was being hurt I would stop this. OK?"

"I only want you safe," I said.

"I am very safe," my wife said, adding, "And I do not want to stop. I'm half-way through the program."

***

We did not have sex until Sunday night, and she still was sore in spots, muscles aching, she said, and her nipples were much more sensitive than usual. After she said that I paid special attention to them, and for the first time I sucked her nipples much longer, encouraged by her reaction, and for the first time in our marriage Eleanor came from sucking on her nipples.

"Damn, first time that ever happened," I said.

"See, positive effects, huh?" she said.

***

74

Later in the week she asked me to take her shopping. "I want to upgrade my wardrobe, what I have is too fuddy-duddy," she said.

I wasn't sure what she had planned but agreed. In the past our clothes shopping was not what I wanted to do and usually managed to sit it out. This was different.

Eleanor would wander through the stacks while I found a seat near the changing room. I was not expecting the fashion show I received. My wife was clearly finding clothes that were sexy down to bordering slutty. I had wanted her to dress like this for years, but always hit a wall.

The skirts where shorter, the dresses tighter, the tops thinner, even the jeans she liked had a lace panel up the sides. I noticed she was wearing a thong when she tried those on. Even something as simple as a button up blouse she tried on and said as she came out, "I know this is plain but…" she unbuttoned four buttons, opening below her breasts, "I can make it a little hotter. Or like this." As I watched she unbuttoned it all the way down and knotted it under her breasts.

"You like," she asked.

"Love it."

"You approve?"

"You know I do."

We left that afternoon with seven hundred dollars' worth of new wardrobe, none of which she would have worn even away on vacation prior to this "program." Eleanor's confidence in herself was obviously at an all-time peak. Her last outfit was a cream silk blouse and micro mini blue skirt. Her nipples were prominent in the blouse and the sway of her soft braless breasts free under the top was absolutely enticing.

I expected these to be her "hot night out" clothes, more for vacations and special nights. I was surprised when she left the last outfit on, telling the saleswoman, "I'll wear these." I enjoyed the men's eyes following my beautiful—and now openly sexy—wife.

Chapter 10

The next Saturday, Saturday number five of the program, the hours changed to an evening schedule. There was no mention of the changed time from Eleanor. Her new wardrobe choices became clear. I suspected in these evenings my wife would be going out in public in her sexy and sometimes revealing outfits—without me but flaunting her newfound sexuality. But I could only guess, I knew nothing more than Aaron's few emails. Eleanor remained mum.

On the drive over I noticed an increased excitement with Eleanor as we neared Aaron's cabin, and when I stopped, she was in a rush to get inside. As I was turning around to leave, I noticed another car outside the garage, a Dodge Viper, parked almost out of sight behind the house.

When I drove up for the return of my wife at 1 a.m., the driveway illuminated with motion sensor lights as I pulled in. The car I had seen earlier was gone. It was 1:15 a.m. before she emerged. Her long tee was noticeably shorter this time, a little shorter, thinner. She was still bubbly when she got in the car, wired. Wide awake.

"Good time?" I asked.

"Oh my, a spectacular time," she said, "I love you." She kissed me, hard. I could taste the alcohol on her breath. She was still buzzed. "Thank you for going along with this. Get me home baby, I need some good lovin'"

"Damn what a shift from last week," I said.

Eleanor giggled. "Maybe because I still have a good buzz. I need your cock inside me quick," she said. I could not remember her every calling a penis a cock. She couldn't wait. As we turned on the main highway, she grabbed for my belt, unzipped my pants, took out my cock and started blowing me, all the way home, including two stops in well-lit parts of town under the red lights. It never slowed her down.

I was stunned at her forwardness, and amazed. I had dreamed of her doing something like this for years, and now here she was.

At home she was horny, taking the lead, stripping our clothes quickly, pushing me back on the bed and straddling me, her pussy so very warm, as wet as I have ever felt her. With me all the way inside her she stopped her rocking, looking me in the eyes. "Do I feel different?"

"Wetter," I said. "Should you feel different?"

"Leave it at that," she said and started moving on my cock, kissing me, rising up to brush her nipples over my face. "Suck my tits," she said, "fuck my wet cunt. My slutty cunt needs a cock so bad." Explicit words so new coming from her, moving faster and faster, panting as we fucked. Her hands were grabbing my ass as if to pull me deeper inside me, urging me on, moaning under her breath, "Damn I love cock so much, my pussy yearns for dick, fuck me lover."

I was trying my best to hold on. She sensed my getting close. Eleanor was so insistent, riding me hard, begging me to fuck her harder and faster, there was no longer holding out. So looking into my eyes as she did. "You like me slutty? You always wanted me to be slut didn't you," she moaned as she bounced on my cock. She gave a half-laugh and gushed. "You may just get what you want," she said. I had to let go.

"Cum inside me," my wife urged. Eleanor timed her words perfectly as I released my sperm inside her. During my own groaning as I came, I thought I heard her say words that were shocking but erotic. "I am such a slut," my wife moaned.

**

The next day Eleanor still avoided my questioning.

"Talk to me Eleanor," I said. "About last night, what you were saying about being a slut?"

"Nothing to say right now honey, it's all a part of the program to get you what you want and to get me to where I want to be. It's only a little while longer, please give me some time for this," Eleanor said.

I do not think I have ever won an argument with her and this time was no different. "OK," I reluctantly said.

**

I didn't let it go at that. I had it in mind that I would follow her, so I borrowed my friend Eric's car. He met me at a shopping center nearest Aaron's cabin earlier in the day and I drove him home. I told Eric I needed the loan because I had a special

79

mechanic who was going to do quick job on my car that evening, and he worked on side jobs only after a full day at the Ford dealership.

I had scoped out a logging road in which I could stay out of sight between Aaron's cabin and the main road, I planned to follow them, discreetly, and at least satisfy my curiosity.

After dropping off my wife, I rushed to the shopping center, traded cars and made a beeline for the logging road. I had only backed into my concealment for a second before Aaron's car flashed by. I waited until they turned the curve before I pulled out and followed them for a mile when a stake bed farm truck pulled out between Aaron and Eleanor and myself, and I lost them at the forks.

My fall back position was to find them by tracking Eleanor's phone, but when I checked it was clear she had left her phone at Aaron's cabin. It hit me that if I was discovered it would not go over well with Eleanor, so I gave up.

***

The sixth and seven Saturdays were carbon copies of the fifth, I would deliver her to Aaron, drink as much as I dared at home before time to drive to pick her up, my mind full of wild and crazy debauchery with my wife as the central focus, truly becoming a slut under Aaron's guidance, but it was only imagination, and what words she had let slip in moments of orgasmic passion. I had no facts.

80

I would be sitting in Aaron's drive for him to return Eleanor to me, although the sixth time instead of the 1 a.m. scheduled time, or the 1:15 of the previous week, it was 1:25. The seventh week even longer. I was outside over 35 minutes before she came to the car. Eleanor made no mention of the delay.

***

And then, just like that, the last Saturday came. I dropped her off a couple of hours early, a last-minute change to 10 a.m. Aaron requested. I was asked to return at five in time for dinner, dressy casual.

81

Chapter 11

At home I checked my email and there was a long attachment from Aaron. I wondered if I would have time to finish it before it was time to leave for dinner, but I started reading. It read:

"Congratulations, Brett, your wife finishes her course tonight. It is the culmination of all those weeks of training, and a demonstration of her accomplishments.

After the exceptional patience you have exhibited, tonight it is all explained. I understand it has not been easy to deliver your wife to me each week and hear nothing back but silence on what is occurring with your wife. Now it is time to let you know what has happened, and the reasons behind taking the steps we did.

I shall break this down in different segments, chronologically.

Prologue:

Eleanor gave me her number at the wedding. I texted asking for her email, as I knew she could copy those if you wanted to read them at some point. She did not feel it proper to talk to me on the phone without your knowledge, but something you could read later she felt was better. A woman's thoughts leading up to beginning this course often helps some husbands in the adjustment period after the completion.

We talked openly about how much we enjoyed each other's company and after a little coaxing, of our almost magnetic attraction to each other. She relayed your reaction and things you said to her on the way home from the wedding, and over the next few exchanges your wife gave me a rather detailed history of your lives, more in depth on the sexual side, because I asked, and because from what I determined from our conversation and observation, this was the area of your lives that could utilize the most improvement—and such programs are one of the programs my company does and is expanding.

With that in mind that I arranged our dinner, with the dancing. Everything that happened than night was discussed with Eleanor prior to that night, primarily to test you on the sincerity of what you were asking of your wife. She wants very much to give you what you asked, but had concerns about your jealously, and her guilt, and inhibitions, while maintaining unshakeable conviction of not harming your marriage. She knew what she wanted but was unsure how to get here. Her own reasoning was in the way. This is often the case.

With that in mind I made you the offer of the program, the one in which Eleanor has already said she wanted to try. "Only eight weeks," is how she said it. I did not correct her, but I think you will see a dramatic change in your wife tonight.

One of the reasons for the silence is to allow your wife to progress without outside influences,

83

without worrying about you judging events without a grasp of the total program. You have handled that part of it admirably.

Saturday 1

The first Saturday Eleanor and I spent the first few hours drinking Mimosas and I outlined part of the program, told her what was expected of her, and quizzed her again on her goals. She wants to fulfill all your fantasies, but it was not until that morning, after much encouragement that she reluctantly opened up and expressed fantasies of her own, some that she said she has never admitted to you—as she was afraid you might be shocked or repelled. You have a nasty hot little wife on your hands, my friend, and you didn't even know it.

After lunch we knew we would be working on a couple of things. first, overcoming her modesty with confidence, and second, per your fantasy, and as I convinced her the first day--her fucking someone else, and in this instance, I was lucky enough to be at the right place at the right time.

In order to get the guilt angle out of the way the solution was simple. I explained as a condition of the program when she walked through my door, she was no longer married—you had given her to me, delivered her, and until I returned her, she was mine. I owned her. I was asking no more than for her to yield to me during the hours she was with me.

Eleanor was required to do as I said, without hesitation, without question, no matter the request. At

84

any moment she could say no and use the safe word I gave her, and the program would cease totally, but by her yielding initial control to me, she was relieving herself of any guilt, as it was not her fault what might happen, but mine. Thus, nothing could ultimately be her fault, I explained. She was happy to agree to this.

I tested her immediately. I told her to strip before lunch, and to eat with me in the nude. She did. I asked her to remove her wedding rings, which she did, placing them in a small box in the foyer table drawer that was there for that purpose, as she would do every time thereafter.

I had her stand in front of a full-length mirror and asked her a series of questions.

"Your height and weight?"

5' 6", 127 pounds."

"Do you think you are height; weight proportionate?" I asked.

"I would like to be thinner," she said.

"Look again," I said. "99 percent of the men in the world would call you perfect. You will admit that, won't you?" She paused but finally nodded. "You do not want to think I would lie, do you?" She shook her head no.

"You have a model's face by anyone's standards," I said. "Look in the mirror, wide set eyes, high cheekbones, expressive eyes, classic perfect nose, full lips. A beautiful woman."

"I've been told that," she said.

"Tell yourself and stop trying to evade it, accept it. Now take a minute, look at yourself. No more lies to yourself," I said.

"I'm very pretty," she admitted.

"Now look at your body," I told her. *"You have a dancer's legs."*

"I have good legs," Eleanor admitted.

"No, you have spectacular legs, and you do know it. Admit it."

"OK, I have great legs," Eleanor said. She was smiling by this point.

"Your waist is not a wasp waist, or do you look emaciated, but you look like a woman, your waist is much smaller than your hips, or your tits, a nice curved near perfect shape. Right? You do not have a muffin top; your belly is remarkably flat considered you have borne two children. Exceptional. Right?"

"My waist is OK, I guess."

"Eleanor, stop this lying to yourself. You've been in dressing rooms with other women, you've been at the beach. You know."

"OK, I have a nice waist," she said.

"Turn sideways," I said. *"And look at your cute tight ass. So perfect anyone in front of you wants to cup it and pull you tight against them."*

"I'll take your word for it; I cannot see behind myself."

"Bullshit, you know you have a cute ass."

"OK."

"Now look at your tits," I said. *"Put your hands underneath them, heft them, look how soft and white they are, the thin veins tinting a tiny blue streak here*

86

and there. Look how they hang, the excellent shape. From their size a soft natural drop, not sagging."

"OK, I have nice tits."

"Size?"

"36 C."

"Back up," I said. She moved back a few steps. "Now walk toward the mirror, watch your tits sway with your steps, like a symphony of movement." She did and smiled as she watched herself. Eleanor stopped short of the mirror.

"Concentrate on your nipples," I told her. "Look how nice and round, brown areola's large." I handed her an old silver dollar. "Hold this against your nipple." I told her. She did. "See, you have heard of men describing perfect silver-dollar sized nipples, look, yours are a little larger than that. Could they be any better?"

"I like my nipples," she said. I noticed that her nipples were hardening into tight buds.

"Look at your nipples themselves, larger than a pencil eraser, perfectly proportioned to your areolas, which are perfect proportioned to your tits."

"OK."

"Now look at the beautiful total woman you are in the mirror. All those exceptional body parts combine to be you. See yourself for what you are. It is a crime to deny others in this world to not enjoy your beauty. You do not wear short skirts to show off your awesome legs, you go to the beach in a one-piece suit that covers your belly and tits. I bet you have few tops and dresses that are low-cut enough to show off your spectacular tits." I watched her face. I knew the

answer. "Why do you cover up what most people would praise your for, that would delight in the visibility of your long legs, your full tits, and the rest. You do not walk around with a bag over your head because you are beautiful, do you?"

"No. That's silly."

"I agree," I said. "Just as silly is being ashamed and shy to cover your amazing assets. Men enjoy seeing you, you should revel in the confidence of your looks. You are beautiful outside. Everyone knows you are beautiful inside. You are the total beautiful package. Everyone knows that—but you."

"If you say so," Eleanor said.

"No. It is a fact. And from this moment forward you will understand that and act accordingly?" She hesitated. "I'll give you two weeks of an assignment to come around to that frame of mind. Every day I want you to stand nude in front of a mirror and go through what we have reviewed." She said she would.

I had made sandwiches prior to her arrival. She did not hesitate to remain nude. Eleanor was nervous at first, but after an hour the shock of nudity eased, and she became comfortable in her own skin, if you will. I made no sexual advance at this time, letting her adjust to the situation.

After lunch we had more drinks and intimate conversation about her goals, your fantasies, and I put on some music and we danced. You've watched us dance, so you know how that was, only with her nude it was many more times intimate. I removed my shirt, and we dance like that for a while, her breasts pressed against my bare chest. I asked her to remove my pants, and she did, and we danced like that, both nude, and we kissed, fondled each other, I dipped my finger into her very wet pussy, and when I touched her clit it was like a little shock went through her each time I pressed it hard. I ordered Eleanor to pull down my boxers, and when she did, without prompting she was on her knees sucking my cock.

I quickly discovered that despite your wife being a talented cocksucker, she was unfamiliar with deep throating and it took some working with her, my hand on the back of her head with my cock hard against the back of her throat, and a lot of her gagging before we made any progress. Not complete the first Saturday but progress all the same.

I led her to the bedroom to fulfill your – and her fantasy. I have never fucked a woman with a warmer, wetter pussy. She was so ready and eager. Eleanor was so ready and enthusiastic when I entered her the first time, with a rewarding smile and kiss.

I had no idea she is multi-orgasmic, and it took coaxing before she learned she no longer had to be quiet and hold what she was feeling inside. I taught her it is OK to be loud, to release the dirty words she held inside, to tell me exactly how bluntly and specifically she wanted to fuck. I made her cum until her legs were too weak to stand. She responded eagerly to my fucking, giving me control, begging me to fuck her harder, to take her.

I pulled her to the edge of the bed and insisted that she tell me exactly what she wanted me to do. She tried to say put my penis inside her, but I refused.

She begged until I gave her the key, using the right words, "stick your cock in my pussy." And so, my friend, that first Saturday afternoon you know for certain that your wife has fucked another man. What you may know now is that she loved it, so much that we rested, and she asked me to fuck her again. She got on top this time.

Afterward we talked of more fantasies, both yours and hers, although it took some probing for her to admit, and a second-long conversation to dig deeper and learn what she was holding back. I spent a long time reinforcing that keeping things unsaid inside her head would not be healthy, how important was that she free her mind of everything she was holding back, afraid to say, embarrassed to admit to me, and to herself. Slowly I began coaxing some of her innermost sexual thoughts and fantasies.

Eleanor seemed relieved to vocalize them for the first time. I am sure some of them will surprise you, but that you will find extremely erotic as well. It became more evident that for Eleanor to make the most progress we should concentrate on her fantasies first—and many of yours would occur as we pursued Eleanor's fantasies.

Your wife was instructed to get her pussy waxed in the next week and keep it that way. She was to no longer wear a bra and would bring all her bras to me with the next meeting, where we would symbolically burn them and burning her inhibition of being shy about her breasts freeing them to move naturally under her clothing.

To reinforce this, I also added bookmarks on her phone to several books and research showing how there is a direct length to breast cancer and wearing bras. "Dressed to Kill" is one of those books. She will not be wearing bras under any circumstance in the future. I trust you noted that rather quickly.

Eleanor also learned that as a part of demonstrating my ownership of her in our time together, she was to strip in the foyer upon arrival, leave her clothes there, remove her wedding rings as for the day she was giving up her wife status, and she would remain nude during the entire time. I also instructed her to continue taking her birth control non-stop to ensure she did not get her period in the middle of the program. She agreed to it all, enthusiastically.

One gauge of how you feel of learning of what your wife did on this first Saturday is how hard your cock is right now. Continue reading, I assure you it will get harder.

This was the first week, there are six more I will describe here, and you will live part of the last session tonight.

***

I took a break, sitting there in front of my computer with a cold sweat. I had to have a drink. As I walked away from the computer it struck me that this was only the first Saturday Aaron had described. I had seven more to go.

Chapter 12

Saturday 2

I explained to Eleanor in our talk phase that morning , over drinks, when she arrived of the importance of opening to her fantasies, and how I planned to push and exceed her boundaries. I fucked her, of course, soon after her arrival. She was less tense this week, much more relaxed and said she had been looking forward to my bedding her all week. The eagerness and enthusiasm she displayed when she was underneath me showed me she had not exaggerated. "I love how you fuck me," she screamed as she was cumming the first time.

Eleanor has understood that in my presence she did not have a vagina or breasts, but tits, a pussy, a cunt, that was made for dicks and cocks. There were no misunderstandings when she uses those terms. There is no love making, it is pure fucking, instinctive, raw. I explained that if we were both raised in the wilds, with no education, and were thrown together, the one natural thing we would do would be to fuck, as all animals do. It is natural for a man and a woman to do that.

Part of her confidence building is understanding her appeal to other men and recognize how sexy and hot she is. Men know, I do not think she realized it, at first but we worked on that.

I had her stand in front of the mirror again and told her to describe herself as she really was, as what she saw now after our previous session and her daily exercise of this."

Eleanor had made great progress in her confidence. "I have a beautiful face, a nice body with pretty tits capped with exceptional nipples. I have been blessed with a tight body, cute ass, and long shapely legs. I am not ashamed of this and will dress in the future to accent my features, to show off my legs and cleavage. I like the feeling of my tits moving naturally as I walk. I am not ashamed if my tits moving under my top makes my nipples hard. It is natural. Men enjoy looking at me. I enjoy men looking at me."

"Very good," I said. "You are accepting these things about yourself quicker than I expected."

One exercise she did that day was to fill out a profile on Match.com, and Tinder, plus a couple of more specific swinger/hotwife sites. I also outlined some parameters on some clothing I would be buying for her for when we would go out, with an eye toward allowing her to better display her overall beauty.

To finish the afternoon took a less courteous approach, more demanding, starting with a light spanking to make the flesh of her ass more sensitive. I blindfolded her, tied her spread to the bed, took a small soft leather multi-strap flail and teased her pussy with it, brushed her body with a feather, ice, the flail, in random patterns. I began asking her in detail about her wildest fantasies, the ones she had never admitted to anyone, the ones she dared not think herself, to let go and say it. Whether she felt ice, a feather, or a flail depended on whether I felt she was telling the truth. She was soon opening her innermost thoughts and fantasies without hesitation, looking deep inside her being, seeking her innermost desires.

I am sure you want to know what those are, and you will, but not here. Keep reading and see how things evolved that allowed her to realize fantasies of her own.

I got her off a half dozen times that Saturday, with various vibrators, dildoes, and finally with me fucking her, along with extremely specific name calling. She will be bringing those toys home with her.

You might want to know that I also showed her a negative test results for various STDs and aids, as she admitted that she prefers her partner to cum inside her pussy, that she considers sex not 100% complete until her lover's cum is inside her.

When we finished fucking I had her stand in front of the mirror and watch my cum dripping from her pussy on to the towel I had laid at her feet.

In the late afternoon to conclude the day I insisted she sit opposite me in the living room, spread her legs with and using her fingers masturbate to orgasm in front of me. As I suspected but she did not confess, being watched doing nasty things is an unstated hotter angle. She squirted when she came. Amazing.

Much of the direction of where this program goes is in many ways directed by Eleanor's ability to open up about her desires and fantasies.

Before she walked out the door to you, I reminded her that she could say no, or the safe word, and this all could end. If not, when she walks in the door next Saturday, she becomes mine, my sexual toy, I own her for those hours, if she wanted. She kissed me and told me this was exactly what she wanted. I told her we were going up a step the next week.

*** *** ***

I determined I needed to pause between each week's narrative, to catch my breath and to prevent an emotional and sensory overload. The liquor helped. I had more days to read about, so I tried to pace myself.

Saturday 3

Upon her arrival on the third Saturday, I had drinks ready, and with her clothes in a heap in the foyer, naked, and much less modest and shy than her first Saturday, we talked more about where she was in the program, the mental exercises of the previous week, what had changed in her thinking.

I had a hairdresser and makeup artist that I use on hand, and they took about an hour to get Eleanor ready. I gave her a robe to cover herself while they were there, but intentionally the robe was very short and did not meet in the middle when she belted it around her. She was tugging in one area and uncovering in another. There was a reason. Finally, she gave up and quit tugging, and discovered that the

95

make-up artist and the hairdresser made no notice that one breast was exposed.

After those two were paid and left, I asked one of my business partners, Jerome, to come into the room from downstairs. Jerome was introduced as the photographer for today. He was fully clothed, and announced the studio set-up was prepared downstairs, with a backdrop and props.

I explained that today we would be taking photos of her, boudoir photos and a few nudes. "Who will see them?" she asked.

"Whoever I wish to see them," I said, adding, "Me, your husband, and maybe a few other people. Enough to let you understand the world does not end when someone sees your beautiful body. With a beautiful package of yours it is a shame to keep it covered most of the time," Eleanor nodded, but I knew this was another wall we must break through.

Brett, you will receive a 12-month calendar with the best 12 photos from the shoot, by the way. We shot for a couple of hours, with drinking, some rather mundane shots, such as Eleanor with one of my dress shirts unbuttoned all the way down, which we used for her online profiles, to total nudes of her touching herself.

I watched for a few minutes and left Eleanor and Jerome alone once they got started. Glamour photos seem to work better that way. I brought in sandwiches and drinks for lunch and noticed the lights in the room were hot. After we ate, I suggested to Jerome there was no need to stay fully clothed, and he agreed as he quicky stripped down to his boxers.

One of the fantasies your wife admitted that she has been holding in, and far up on the list, is a curiosity and fantasy of being with well-built tall black man. Jerome at 6' 4" fits this exactly, dark black skin which she had said was a plus, and while he is my primary photographer, he was perfect for his role this day.

Eleanor has been shooting nudes for 20 minutes or so after lunch, well into the drinking, Jerome had been directing her casually, subtly, and she was facing him, her legs spread wide, touching her pussy. He asked her to spread her pussy lips apart and show how wet she was, and she did. Eleanor was breathing heavily, her eyelids were half closed, and I noticed that Jerome was sporting a huge hard on.

I walked over to Eleanor, her legs still spread open and told her she should feel free to enjoy Jerome and fulfill her fantasy today. I am not ordering you to fuck him, but I would like for you to, and I think you want to. I think you will."

"I will," she said, and without hesitation added, "I want to." I moved out of the way, standing at the door as she did not move her position, but motioned with her finger for Jerome to come closer to her. He moved between her open legs and kissed her, and I gave them their privacy. I was barely out of the door when I heard your wife scream, "Oh my God."

For the next 45 minutes the house was echoing with the sounds of your wife being blacked for the first time, as I edited photos from the shoot from the SD card on my computer.

Jerome is a little rough sometimes, and I wanted him to be with her, as I know she had never been fucked like that before, by someone who was taking her pussy, and I did hear some pops and yelps as he fucked her hard. When the sounds quieted down, I went back downstairs.

Eleanor was laid back on the couch, sweating, her face flushed crimson, and her legs open, cum pouring from her pussy. Jerome was a few feet away taking photos of his cum oozing from your wife. She was smiling at the camera.

I knew Eleanor enough by this time to have a strong suspicion how the day would go, and I was not wrong. I made it a point to tell Jerome to take some portraits of your wife's face at different times in the day: when they started on the photos, when the session heated up, right before he started to fuck her, and finally after he had finished fucking her that first time, for another portrait.

You'll get copies of those, and the visible transition between the photos is amazing, the innocence to the anticipation to the fulfilled and amazed. It is almost as if they are photos of three different women. The last one, after she has gone black is the most interesting, her eyes, you can see in her eyes what is to come, and her determination to go there.

I asked them to come upstairs and noticed as she went to the restroom a trail of cum was running down the inside of her leg.

I asked Eleanor to go to my computer and check her responses to the online ads and respond to any that interested her. I showed her the photos and she selected two, one with her in a shirt unbuttoned to her waist, and the other with her completely topless, her hands under her tits as if offering them to the camera. She spent 15 minutes at the computer, before standing, taking Jerome by the hand, and leading him back downstairs where they had fucked earlier, and soon there was more moaning and screaming as they fucked again.

I checked the computer. Every person to who she had responded was black. Two of the men had been sent the topless shots.

We all moved upstairs to the bedroom, drinking, all nude, and Eleanor seeing her sexuality in a whole new way. I explained we were going for a lot of firsts, and she was excited at the prospect.

This is the day your wife first enjoyed allowing two men inside her body at the same time, and her first double vaginal penetration, and the first time she experienced a double penetration, although it was with me enjoying her ass for the first time. With Jerome it would have been an impossibility. When she finished as we rested Eleanor exclaimed, "That was the most unbelievable fucking of my life."

"You know this is only the beginning, don't you?"

"Yes, I want to try it all," she said. "I how no idea how freeing this is." She was pensive for a moment. "Do you think this is the way Brett wanted me to be?"

"What do you think?" I asked.

"I think it is."

I told her that she had earned the title of slut now, and she admitted, "I am a slut and added without prompting, "and I love it."

Chapter 13

Holy shit, I said aloud. Eleanor had never given me any indication that she was interested in black men. The shock was one thing. I already had a buzz from drinking as I read Aaron's description of my wife's previous Saturdays, despite my pacing myself.

I was overwhelmed. I took a break and stepped outside to get air and sit by the pool. I had a yearning desire to hear my wife's voice, to talk to her, but that would not happen. I had delivered her to Aaron today, and obviously now, to whomever he might decide to share her with.

It took a while to process that thought, but the image of my wife on her back with her legs spread while a black man with a big cock was plunging in and out of her pussy was stuck in my head. One of the thoughts that flashed inside my head was, I wonder if they videoed it.

Was this what I really wanted? Were we in too deep to draw back? I realized my cock was rock hard.

I felt I needed to take a longer break from reading Aaron's narrative, to process more of what had happened to my wife, but then again it had happened weeks early, it is only now that I am discovering the facts. I wondered how she could go through these sexual changes and adventures and conceal it from me, without giving me even give me a hint, and how she maintained the façade of my innocent housewife at home—when she was moving faster to a slut stage on these Saturdays. After a while I was drawn back into Aaron's narrative.

I took the time to jerk off to the image in my mind of my new slutty wife.

Saturday 4

This was amazing progress in only three weeks. Your wife is finally embracing her beauty, her sexuality, and opening herself to a wider variety of sexual possibilities—all of which you said you wanted—but more, now exploring what she wanted.

We were over the big hurdles now, but we were still ensuring that this is not a temporary change but is to the point that her newly discovered sexuality comes naturally, without thought, without doubt.

The direction of the program so far has been building your wife's self-confidence, overcoming her reluctance to fulfill your fantasies and help Eleanor become more of a woman you want at this stage of your life together. An important part of this is Eleanor fulfilling her own fantasies as well.

This was all in mind as she arrived for her fourth Saturday, the last session from 8 until 6. Saturday five begins the evening schedule.

An indication of Eleanor's frame of mind at this point was when she arrived. I was in the kitchen, intentionally, and heard her enter. When I entered from the kitchen, she was standing in the living room, naked. I greeted her. She looked around. "Is Jerome here today?" she asked.

"Do you want him to be?" I asked.

"Yes, I had hoped."

"You want to fuck him again?"

"Yes," your wife said.

"He will be here later," I said, and she smiled a wide smile.

"Good," she said.

We spent much of the morning reviewing more photos which Jerome had shot of Eleanor the previous Saturday, and at my suggestion she picked out more photos for the profiles, updated her photos on Match and Tinder with a sexier clothed shot, and on additional photos in each profile, in the areas that she could choose who saw her topless or nude, she loaded photos for those.

Eleanor answered responses of the ones that struck her fancy and gave access to her topless shots to a couple more, and two of the most enticing responses she gave access to her nude shot.

"How do you feel about other men seeing you naked, wanting you, getting turned on."

"I think it is hot," she said, and smiled. "Why don't you check," she said. I pulled her to my lap and probed her pussy with a finger.

"You are soaking," I said. "You need some cock?"

"You know I do," she said.

Leading her to the bedroom, I tied her hands and ankles to the corners of the bed, blindfolded her, and did nothing for four or five minutes. It was clear she was anticipating whenever I would brush her body and she would jerk, but I only teased.

103

What I did was go to a new toy, a suction tube that I placed on each nipple and twisted the knob that sucked air away from the entrance, pulling her nipple inside the large tube. I did the other the same way, twisting a little and sucking more of each nipple inside the tube. I left them in place as I used a vibrator and made her cum, with a dildo inside her pussy as I did.

I left her in that position and left her tied on the bed and blindfolded, anticipating what was next. Jerome texted that he was outside, so I quietly let him into the house, explained that Eleanor was tied to the bed upstairs and was waiting on him to fuck her, and asked him to fuck her without speaking or letting her know exactly who it was, and then after he came to leave the room.

I watched as he did just that, rubbing her pussy, fingering her, and removing the tubes from her nipples, kissing them with much more sensitivity from the tubes, and her nipples were enlarged and puffy from the treatment. She came twice while Jerome fucked her. He left the room, and I let her rest a minute before I do went in and fucked her without speaking.

Again, we left her tied to the bed, Jerome and I went downstairs and had a drink, comparing notes about how delightful it was to fuck your wife, how exciting she was responding to everything, and talking about how the slut side of your wife was emerging.

After the drink I went upstairs, removed the blindfold, untied her. She needed to go to the restroom, and from the cum dripping from her I told her there was disposable douches under the sink. When she came back into the bedroom she asked, "Who fucked me?"

"Does it matter?" I said, "I shared your pussy that loves cock. You have been shown that a cock in your pussy, even if you do not know who it is, it is still pleasurable. And the world keeps spinning, doesn't it? Nothing really changed except you got fucked," I said.

"Yes, I did," she smiled. "And you are right, to a slut it should not matter, should it?"

"I think you are starting to understand more about your sexual inner being than you did," I said. "So what do you think about being fucked and not even knowing who it was?"

"It is hot. Thank you," Eleanor said.

Eleanor was excited to see Jerome waiting downstairs, and she understood then that her stranger lovers had been Jerome and myself. She was not through with Jerome, however, and took him back to the bedroom for the afternoon. I left it to the two of them. They were loud and vocal.

***

Saturday 5

The reason the times shifted to Saturday nights after four sessions is by now obvious to you, I suspect. It is time for the new Eleanor to emerge in public. Your wife is now releasing most of her

105

inhibitions, fulfilling fantasies of yours, and hers, and has discovered the journey thus far is exciting beyond anything she has ever experienced. The week between sessions gives her time to keep one foot solid in her everyday life, to reassure that it remains and is still hers, as well as her now opened slut side, which is hers as well.

Jerome and I were waiting when she arrived, stripped in the foyer, and seemed confused for a second where she should sit, eventually taking a seat beside Jerome on the couch. I told her that she had clothes laid out on the bed and to please change.

On the bed was the outfit you chose, the lowcut cowl neck with the open back, a micro mini skirt, black lace thong, and black high heels, large ghetto hoop earrings. From her consultation with the make-up artist on her photography day, she added large smoky eyes and bright red lipstick. When she entered the living room, she exuded sex, beauty, with a hint of slutty, as if it was smoldering inside her, ready to burst into flame.

Eleanor asked where we were going, and I said simply, "Out. I think it is time we showed you off." She shrugged and together the three of us went to my car, making small talk while I drove to a club I had previously selected, something of a meat market for the late 30's crowd.

We pulled up at the club, and I told her to go in ahead of us, that we were here to reinforce in her mind how attractive she is to men, how her self-confidence should be reinforced. I also told her that before we left, I wanted her to obtain the phone

106

numbers of three different men. She went in smiling, her shoulders back, tits out and bouncing with each strong step, a broad smile, and the most confident air I have seen her exhibit.

Jerome and I waited five minutes before we entered. Eleanor was seated at the bar, her back toward the door, and that expanse of bare back causing almost anyone to catch their breath. She was stunning. A tall black man with dreads was chatting her up, and as I watched she handed him her phone and he added his number. The continued chatting and she said something, he nodded, kissed her cheek and moved away.

The exchange and dread's exit had not gone unnoticed. She was nursing her drink, checking her phone, and texted me. "One down." No black man in the room has missed that she was being receptive to a black man, and another black man approached, stocky, broad shoulders, tight black tee showing off his body builder frame. From their body language he is a smooth player, nodding, smiling, and Eleanor was responding to the attention, brushing back her hair, leaning forward toward him giving him a great view of her tits, flirting to the max. He put his arm around her back, and she did not resist. When he started moving toward her tit, she stopped him, gave him a warm smile, and she handed her cell to him, where she entered her number. He drifted away. "No. 2" she texted.

I was shocked when a white guy came in, glanced around the room and went straight to Eleanor. She smiled, stood and gave him a hug. He was smiling back, gave her a buss, and that was when I recognized him. It was Eric from the wedding in Florida. I did not arrange it, but however it happened he was here.

Eleanor and Eric moved to an empty table, ordered a bottle of wine, and she texted. "I already have his number, I think this counts though, don't you?"

"We'll see," I texted back.

"I think we are going outside for a few minutes to get some air, I'll be back," she said. As soon as she put the phone down, Eric stood, helped her up, and the two of them walked outside. I left Jerome holding the table, stepped outside, standing in the shadows, and saw Eleanor and Eric climbing into the back of a small, customized transit van camper. I was not outside long before I saw the camper rocking. I went back inside and told Jerome what was happening, explaining about them meeting earlier at the wedding.

"Girl is starting to like strange cock, isn't she?" he asked. She was outside 45 minutes, came back into the bar a bit disheveled, hair mussed, the cowl neck a little crooked, hardly any lipstick, and she made her way to the restroom, coming back to the bar with everything back in place. I knew she had been fucked, but no one could tell from her outward appearance. There was a seat open at the bar and she took it, in no hurry to leave. Eric did not reenter the bar.

A third black man approached, older, with a beard, taking the seat beside her and introducing himself. They talked for 10 minutes, he was touching

108

her leg, and as she was looking into his face, she spontaneous reached her hand behind his head and pulled her to him for a kiss. She broke it, they talked for a minute more, and she took out her phone, typing the number he gave her, and punching send. She stood and he kissed her again, pulling her tight, his hand half under her cowl neck from the side, before he broke away with a grin. He whispered again and she nodded, backing away a foot or so and lifting her top above her tits, giving him a good view of her pretty tits. She was giggling as she pulled her top down.

Eleanor was typing into her phone and I received her text. "I have three black men's phone number and I've been fucked. I am ready for something else," she said.

Jerome and I took her back to my place, and I backed away from my participation this night. It was clear that Jerome was her primary sexual interest, she was fired up from the attention of the black men in the bar and I didn't want her distracted. She was in a black cock mood.

Your wife has discovered her confidence, ridding herself of her modesty, and had learned of the effect she has on men, and the ability she owns to lure them closer. She was also accepting and understanding her developing preference for black cock. I picked up on it after fucking Eric she wanted to stay and get the number of another black man.

At one point from the bedroom, I heard Jerome demanding of Eleanor, "You like black cock?" She was screaming her answer at the top of her voice.

"I love black cock, I love it. Do not ever stop fucking my white cunt."

"What will you do for me?"

"Anything, everything, I will do it all," Eleanor screamed.

When they finished, she barely had time to get a shower before your arrival.

Saturday 6

From my conversations with Eleanor over the previous Saturdays, and our email exchanges through the week, I was understanding what the best way would be to give you what you wanted, what she says she wanted, entering a new level of sensuality for your continued life together, to become an open, uninhibited, sensual sexy woman. Guiding her is best handled by following your wife's desires and fantasies rather than what I think. The momentum is vital, and it is natural for her want more of what she prefers, the path of least resistance.

For that reason, when she arrived, stripped, and put her wedding rings in the foyer drawer, Jerome was there waiting too. I asked her to go to the bedroom and put on what was laid out there for her to wear (the lace dress in the catalog illustration I sent), Jerome was taking her out tonight.

"You aren't going?"

"No," I said. "Jerome is going to show off his white snowbunny tonight. Everyone you see tonight will know that he will be fucking you before the night is over. Does that excite you?"

110

"You know it does, we've talked about it," your wife told me. And we had, one of her fantasies she admitted was to be shown off by a black man as his white woman.

I did stay behind, but I knew what was planned, which Jerome later confirmed. They went to dinner in a nice restaurant, with Eleanor wearing an unbuttoned vest over the open weave lace dress. She wore a black thong underneath it, and black high heels.

After their dinner it was early, and Jerome took her to an adult bookstore, remaining outside and telling her to go inside and select a number of items for which he gave her the cash to buy. She was to pick out an interracial CD they could watch later that night, and a realistic black dildo, and to not take one with the idea of getting in and out but to browse and pick out something only after five minutes. She was out in 10 minutes and handed the bag to Jerome. She has selected a video featuring two black men one white woman video, and a large black realistic rubber dick. She continued to wear the vest, concealing her breasts for the most part.

Jerome drove them to a predominately black club for dancing, another reason I wasn't along, white men do not fit in there, and on the drive, Eleanor mentioned that one man offered her a handful of tokens if she wanted to go into the private boxes in the back and watch them. She asked why he would do that, and Jerome explained that once she had gone into the booth, men would go into the booths on the other side of hers, and stick their cocks

111

through the holes, where she was supposed to jerk off or suck their cocks. She didn't believe him at first, but Jerome told her he would take her back to the store and prove it, he'd take her into one of the booths, but she would have to suck the cock that came through the glory hole.

Your wife's response, "Another time. Not tonight."

As I said, Jerome is an associate in my program training, and he understands it is an important to change plans as input from the client adds more information. They continued to the black club, he danced with her in a very forward manner, felt her up as they were dancing, got some drinks in her, and she was hot. "She was ready to fuck in the car in the parking lot," Jerome said, "but I told her we were not thought yet." The club was hot, and at Jerome's request Eleanor removed the vest, even though her nipples were visible through the open weave. She was nonchalant about her exposure.

Jerome drove to another club, "Tophats" a strip club near Atlanta, and took her inside, where they had more drinks, and Eleanor was curiously watching the goings on around the room, the table dances, the girls onstage, the reaction of the men in the club. Jerome said that how Eleanor was dressed in the open lace and her breasts showing so much that they blended in, that most of the men probably thought Eleanor was working.

A dancer came and sat with them and asked if your wife was there to audition. Apparently Tophats is always looking for talent, and a couple of times a month they advertise for dancers, with those nights set up for women to get up on stage and strip as a part of applying for the job.

Jerome, playing to the moment, slipped the dancer a c-note and asked her to help get your wife on stage for a set.

Remember that Eleanor is already drinking, hot from dancing in the club, being felt up in public, the stimuli of the adult bookstore, so it wasn't a stretch for Jerome to encourage her to do it as a confidence builder.

The dancer danced for Eleanor, touching her, getting your wife that much hotter, and encouraging Eleanor to try going on stage. After some more encouragement from Jerome and the dancer, she let the dancer lead her into the dressing room.

Eleanor did a three-song set, using a costume borrowed from the dancer and was a hit with the customers, several asking to buy table or lap dances which she refused. She was further complimented by the manager actually offering her a job, which she declined.

Eleanor was so horny from exposing herself on stage in front of everyone that she insisted that Jerome fuck her in the car in the parking lot this time. It was only starters, as Jerome took her to his place, which was close by, where they watched the movie, she fucked herself with the black rubber dick as Jerome watched, and they fucked again. She showered there, and barely made it back in time to be picked up by you.

I understand this may have gone further than you anticipated, but please understand this has been guided at this point by your wife's fantasies. She has achieved all the goals in your mind for her, but she has some of her own to achieve. You wanted a woman sexy and confident of her appearance, could fuck another man for you (and herself), and come back home to a normal life. I think each week you've discovered you have both women you wanted, the domestic wife, and the slut one. Hang on.

You have what you wanted, now she must get what she wanted. Returning to the simple normal life might be more difficult going forward.

Chapter 14

I was running out of time, but there was no way I could leave, or see my wife again without knowing as much of the story as I could obtain. I continued reading for Day 7:

***

Saturday 7

Brett, I am sure you see the steady escalation of the expansion of your wife's sexuality, but I cannot describe in words the enthusiasm that each new challenge or something she has not done before does to heighten her excitement. She is an excitement junkie. That part of her has emerged, and something for which you should be prepared when she completes the program.

Which brings us to the seventh night of the program. What follows is a fantasy that she was hesitant to admit, even more reluctant to admit that she was willing to live out in the right circumstance. You know as a part of the program that we were going to make that happen though, didn't you?

As per the routine, she left her clothes piled in the foyer, her wedding rings in the drawer, and her clothes for the evening laid out on the bed. She asked me, "are you sure?" when she saw the clothes we had laid out, but I assured her we were.

You were only out of sight when Jerome, Eleanor, and I made a beeline for the local private airstrip. One of Jerome's friends owns a private plane charter service, and was there, waiting in the cockpit with the motors turning over. For what was planned we did not want to spend the hour and a half driving. Eleanor took the seat facing toward the tail of the plane, and Jerome and I took the ones facing forward.

In less than 45 minutes we were landing at the executive jet airport in Fulton County. A car was waiting, and we went to dinner at a place recommended by Orneal, the pilot friend of Jerome's. He remained in the cockpit when we landed, securing the plane with plans to catch up later.

We had a light dinner, more drinks, hit a club where she and Jerome danced—it was not the kind of dancing I do or even understand, but your wife took to it quickly, twerking, rubbing her ass on Jerome's cock and calling it dancing, although she had several men try to dance with her Jerome was able to fend them off.

What followed is the most detailed and elaborate evening we could arrange. I have not yet described what your wife was wearing this night, but it was a micro mini skirt, so short that the clefts of both hips were exposed. Underneath the skirt she was wearing a red thong, and black fishnet hose that went up to mid-thigh, connected to the waist band by two long strips of the same material, solid, so it gave the appearance of a pair of garter belt panty hose. Her top was a pale-yellow crop top with the lower hem

116

loose, dropping only a couple of inches below her tits. Her very high heels topped off the outfit.

When she first dressed, she came out tugging at the material that was not tuggable and looking in the mirror. "Damn, I look like a hooker," she said, giggling.

"Tonight you are my hooker, my ho," Jerome said, and they kissed before we left the house. "Say it."

"I'm your whore tonight, at least I'm dressed for it," Eleanor said.

When we left the dance club we drove to the strip, where working girls were strolling up and down the sidewalk. You could hear Eleanor's breath getting heavier when she saw where we were.

"You don't..."

"It's your fantasy," I told her. "Here's your chance. We have a girl that's going to watch over you and give you a pointer or two. Are you willing?"

Eleanor was as excited as I had seen her since this started. This was causing her tremble. "I know this is crazy, but, hell, let's do it," she said. We pulled to the side, and I introduced Eleanor to Tiffany, a girl who had been referred to us and we had talked to the day before, and was working for us tonight, to watch over your wife as she executed her whore fantasy.

What we did not tell Eleanor was that Orneal, the pilot from the plane, who she had not seen as he stayed in the cockpit, had moved into position while we were at the club and was waiting for our text to circle the block, give her a look over, then pick her up on the second circuit. Tiffany was told to look for a silver Escalade that Orneal was driving. I was texting Orneal keeping informed of our progress.

As you can see the plan was to allow your wife to live out her fantasy, as safely but as realistically as we could. Jerome and I dropped her off with Tiffany, who gave her a quick course on how to approach a car, what to say and look for to see if they were cops, and not to get in anyone's car unless she gave Eleanor the nod. Tiffany also told her of the wood rimmed parking lot behind a school a couple of blocks away where it was the best place to go to earn her money.

Jerome and I circled the block, parked across the street where we could watch, and waited. Eleanor attracted a lot of attention. With Tiffany at her side, she walked up to a couple of cars, talked, and flashed her tits at one of the cars as they talked. They had asked to see the merchandise, and your wife was really getting into it, but true to the plan Tiffany pulled her back.

A silver Escalade pulled up with a large black man at the wheel. Tiffany motioned her forward, and the man was leaning over the seat, reaching through the window to get a feel of Eleanor's tits. They talked more and this time Tiffany gave her the nod. Eleanor climbed in. I could see her shaking legs from where we were, as far away as we were. As the Escalade pulled away, I received a text. Orneal said he was tied up, had been pulled over for having a broken taillight, but he would be on in a few minutes.

118

Jerome and I both did an "oh shit", but at this point what could we do? We could have barged down behind the school and maybe broken it up, but then again, we realized the best thing to do was wait. In about 25 minutes the Escalade pulled up and your wife climbed out, smiling, high fiving Tiffany, on a high of excitement, displaying a wad of cash. Eleanor had officially turned a trick. She was now a whore.

Tiffany and Eleanor approached a couple of more cars, flirted, passed, and Orneal finally pulled up. There was some confusion on Tiffany's face when she realized what may have happened, two Escalades, but she recovered quickly, again giving Eleanor the nod, and as planned Eleanor climbed in with Orneal, who also took her to the school lot for thirty minutes.

By now Tiffany figured out that one of the two silver Escalades was a genuine customer buying pussy, not the set-up, and she also realized that while babysitting Eleanor she had missed several tricks of her own, and a regular of hers pulled up. Eleanor was gone, so Tiffany jumped in with the regular went to turn a trick on her own, seeing an opportunity to put more cash on top of what we were paying her.

Orneal pulled to the curb after fucking your wife while parked at the old school and Eleanor exited, looking around for Tiffany but shrugging before moving back from the street where she and Tiffany had been standing. Eleanor moved toward the edge of the sidewalk and started walking back and forth, smiling, making eye contact and waving at a couple of cars that were driving by very slow.

119

I knew she was in the moment and we had to end this, so we pulled up to Eleanor and she was smiling as she approached. "Hey guys, you looking for some company," she said, still in the role, before she saw who we were.

"You ready to go?" I asked. "You have fulfilled your fantasy, twice."

Eleanor was still on the excitement high, and she actually said, "You know, as long as I am here, I might like to try it one more time before we go." I thought we had been lucky enough for one night, and I told her we would need to get started to be sure she we got back in time for you to pick her up. I think that snapped her out of her moment.

Tiffany got out from her trick at that moment, and she came over. Eleanor told her goodbye and thanked her for the advice and help, they hugged, and Tiffany told her she was welcomed to come back and work with her any time.

"Look here," she said, showing a wad of hundreds. "I made $400.00."

Living this fantasy had Eleanor on a high, she was so hot that she was all over Jerome on the way back to the airport. She gave him a blowjob while they rode, telling him not to worry, she had used condoms with her two tricks.

Your wife didn't catch the set-up until she recognized Orneal back at the airport and saw his silver Escalade. She laughed and realized that the other silver Escalade was the real deal. "I did it, didn't I?'

120

"You had a fantasy of wanting to be a whore, guess what? You are now an official whore, you got picked up on the street and turned a trick, twice you thought, but once a genuine prostituting of yourself. Are you OK with it?" I asked.

"Incredibly horny," she said. When we landed, she was still talking about it, and she looked at the clock. *"We really didn't need to get back here this quick, did we?"*

"No, we were trying to keep you safe, we got lucky on the one trick."

"Well we have time for me to realize another fantasy then," she said. I wasn't clear what that was. *"Fucking two black men at once," she said.* She looked up at Jerome and Orneal. *"Are you up for it?"*

I think your wife has learned that men will not turn down the chance to fuck her if they are given that chance, so Orneal returned back to my place with us, and both he and Jerome had a turn with your wife only a little while before your arrival, which explains why she was late coming out.

Brett, you no longer have a shy, modest, uninhibited wife. That is what you wanted. And she had fantasies of her own, including seeing what it would like to be a prostitute. So, when your wife returned to you the night of Saturday, session seven, I returned you a wife, a slut, and a whore.

I am sure you are questioning what is happening today, as you delivered your wife to me early today. She left with Jerome and Orneal, and you will meet me here at five. I'll drive us to dinner, and we will

121

meet up with your wife later tonight. There is evidentially still a fantasy or two yet to fulfill, a fantasy of hers yet to be lived.

On a positive note, after tonight there are no more Saturday sessions, your wife has completed the program with flying colors, you have held up your end admirably. It has been fun participating in this exercise with you.

For your reference my company typically charges $20,000 for the program you have received free, but I was telling the truth when I said I wanted to offer it to you free because you and Eleanor are nice people, I thought you could benefit from the program, and what I did not mention is I could detect the slut side of your wife bottled up inside her and only needing a little guidance to help it explode, and it did. In the end I hope you will enjoy the results.

Of course, there is still tonight to go.

Chapter 15

I stared at the computer screen a long time, checking the time. I had a half-hour before I needed to leave to meet Aaron. One more night. What else could it be? I shuddered a little at the thought, and I was not shuddering from what Aaron and team was doing, because they were doing what my wife fantasized, her fantasies. What I was worried about now is what other fantasies did she have inside that pretty head.

My one consolation was after tonight, this would all be over, and my wife and I could get back to our lives. I hoped. Could our lives be the same again after her programming.

I was at Aaron's at 5 p.m.

***

"Come in, let's have a drink and talk about a few things," Aaron said. "I take it you've read what has occurred these last eight weeks." I nodded and took the drink. The drink shook in my hand. My anger was struggling to burst free and thrash the hell out of this man who, the way I was thinking, had taken my wife and debased her over a series of weeks.

I didn't because I knew I would not stop until I had choked the life out of him, and I had read his version of what had happened. I needed to wait until I heard Eleanor's version, until I had her safely back in my arms. It was like Aaron was reading my mind.

123

"Brett, I am sure at this moment you are angry. This thing went in ways you did not expect, and I admit I did not tell you how things would evolve, or even how I expected them to evolve based on past cases before we started all this, but this was not to your detriment, as you might believe right now," Aaron said. "Please reserve judgement."

"I'm listening," I said.

"We will start with what me paraphrasing our early conversations in which I heard that you wanted. You said you wished for Eleanor to be less inhibited, less modesty, more confident with herself, embracing her sexuality, and open to fulfilling your fantasies. Is that a fair description?"

"Yes, that about sums it up," I said.

"I told you I felt we could achieve this through our 8-week program."

"Yes."

"And after every session, your wife was returned to you, and your normal day to day life was, well, your day to day life, basically unchanged, although you enjoyed an increase in sexual frequency, and some new things you were not expecting, as her learning how to deep throat your cock, with more self-confidence than she had ever had, right?"

"Yes," I said. "But that is not..."

Aaron interrupted. "We quickly achieved what you wanted with breaking through the mental barriers your wife had erected, but for these changes to be reinforced and to keep from sliding back to the older more inhibited ways, we had to go well beyond those

124

limits, so if she regresses a bit, the bulk of our work remains intact. Does that make sense?"

"Yes," I had to admit. "It does."

"One thing that I didn't bring out up front is you are getting what you wanted—but from the very beginning this was all about Eleanor. You had your fantasies. She has hers. You expressed yours to her. Eleanor had never expressed her fantasies to anyone. To get to that point she had to release herself, learn to let go, and as she grew into confidence to go inside herself and admit her own fantasies. She wanted to fulfill them." Aaron said, continuing, "A huge part of releasing her inner slut was to live those fantasies, and within our safe cocoon of this program that was not only possible, but an important part of that moving closer to your wife not only being the sexual person you want her to be, but more important the sexual person that she discovered she can be. You would have objecting to parts of the program, I'm sure. Eleanor has to live out her fantasies before she can even talk to you about them."

This was almost too much to process. "Give me a minute to absorb what you just said," I said, handing him my empty glass which he refilled. I took a drink and told him, "OK, go on."

"Thank you for listening so far," Aaron said. "That reveals much of your progress too. Once she had discovered she could allow someone else's cock inside her and the world didn't end, in fact, as she discovered returning home, little changed in her world, except sexually. In the days that followed it gave her time to reinforce her releasing her

125

inhibitions, express her fantasies, and enjoy the ultimate rush, living her fantasies. Did you know her fantasies?"

"No."

"Neither did I, and her expressing them dictated the direction in which we went. I had always planned to shoot boudoir shots evolving into nudes," he said. "Oh yes, this is yours." Reaching to the night table he showed me a ringed wall calendar, flipping through a couple of the months, each one a full color 11 x 14 photo of Eleanor in a sexy artistic pose. I didn't recognize her at first, she was so glamorous and exotic, and as pretty as any supermodel I have seen. Each month was more revealing. He did not turn to December. As I watched he placed the calendar in a large envelope. "You can take that with you when you leave tonight, we'll leave it here for now." I nodded.

"Jerome is a top photographer, part owner of the company, and of course very large, very black, and was very willing to fuck your wife. Actually I think he is a bit smitten with her. He says he has never fucked anyone else that enjoys fucking the way she does, and of course that combination with Eleanor's personality and natural beauty, well you are a most fortunate man. You need to understand that every man seems to fall a little in love with your wife, and going the further step of fucking her makes it deepen, something I guess we can call a possible negative side effect of the treatment." Aaron smiled. He seemed cocky and enjoy this. I may have been

126

squirming uncomfortably, but my anger was easing. I hated how he was making sense.

"Jerome would never have fucked Eleanor has she not expressed a fantasy of fucking a black man. Same with two men at once. Your wife was the one who wanted to go out in public and be shown off by a black lover, to flaunt to everyone in view that there was no doubt this man would be fucking her before the night was over." Aaron paused to take a pull of his own drink, followed with water.

"The clothing she wore, remember you had input on that, was revealing, of course, a part of helping her overcome her modesty inhibitions. The ultimate display of her confidence was her auditioning at the strip club. My goodness I cannot describe how turned on that made her. 'I owned that room when I was up there naked,' she was gushing when she came back. 'That felt so powerful.' What I am trying to get to is we did not force of these bold steps on her, the program is not that, it evolved into helping her release her fantasies and live them, which in turn allows the releasing of inhibitions and opening up her slut side. I did not know exactly the person we would release with the program, there was no way to predict it—but what has emerged is for sure you have a slut wife, Brett."

"And a whore?" I ventured.

"About that," Aaron said, "That did take a strange turn. As you read our goal was for her to realize her fantasy as safely as possible, but still keep it as real as we could make it for her. No one expected that there would be another man driving the

127

same type of automobile as the one Tiffany was expecting. On the positive side, it turned out safely in the end, and it was not only a set-up scenario. Your wife did whore her pussy, and when we wanted to leave, she wanted to turn one more trick. Yes, she has learned she can explore her fantasies and wants to. And that brings us to tonight."

"Yes."

"I do not know exactly how it goes from here, as it has so far, Eleanor and her reactions and desires are steering things. I know she wanted to go out tonight with Orneal and Jerome, she wants to be shown off by two black men as their black cock slut. She said that much. Other than that we will discover as the evening progresses. I'm expecting a call any minute from Jerome to tell me where to meet them. What I can assure you is that when she is with Jerome, he will take good care of her, watch over her, keep her safe. His responsibility is she is still a part of the program until tonight ends. Do you have any questions?"

I struggled to think of something to ask. "So what happens after tonight," I asked. "How does it go forward."

Aaron laughed. "Good question. The thing is it goes wherever the two of you want it to go. You wanted her open and honest sexually. She is that way now. Throughout all this she has expressed her love for you, how nearly everything in her life is perfect with you and she wants little change in that, and with her opened sexually it is like icing on the cake, is how she termed it. I think it is fair to say that if you

128

are troubled with something she wants to continue, that for the sake of your marriage she will not go there—but you need to understand that by doing so, by being controlling and not embracing this newfound sexual freedom you both enjoy, that you will be regressing from what you said you wanted. In short, your marriage is safe, but that does not mean you should neglect nurturing it, and always trying to go forward. Monogamy is probably history though. It is hard to get that genie back into the lamp."

I felt reassured and was struggling for another question to keep the conversation going. I looked at my watch. It was seven. The phone rang. I could only hear Aaron's side of the conversation. "Yes, we're good, OK, sounds good. No problem. Around 9 then."

Aaron glanced at the clock. "We have a couple of hours to kill, let's get some dinner."

***

Dinner was agonizing and slow. Aaron was relaxed, courteous, keeping the conversation light about sports, stories of his travels, and as usual concentrating on things of my interests that he would determine, places Eleanor and I had visited, what we thought about them, places we would like to go, what we enjoyed most when we were there, restaurants we would recommend, always listening, as if what I was the most interesting thing he had ever heard.

It had taken me until now to understand this was a professional technique, as much as asking a series of questions to which the only answer was "yes" and then when the zinger came, the natural inclination was to say yes to that as well. Not quite propaganda, not quite brainwashing, but certain effective into building trust by attentive listening.

I wondered how much of Aaron was a professional act versus sincerity, and the question nagging in my mind was why he would give away an eight week program that he say he typically charged five figures, claiming on the basis of our being nice people and friendship. No matter how courteous, that didn't wash, and I waited for the other foot to fall on that premise.

Chapter 16

We were back in the car and traveling to yet another destination after dinner, shortly after the top of the hour Aaron pulled into a gentleman's club, "Tophats." I gave him a high eyebrow look.

"I am somewhat as in the dark as you are, this is where Jerome said to meet," Aaron said, looking down, texting on his phone.

"They're running late, let's go in, have a drink, and enjoy the scenery."

There's no denying that I love the atmosphere of a titty bar, having a drink, beautiful women on stage getting naked, bare breasted women standing on a tiny platform in front of you stripping off their tops, everyone smiling, the lights dim enough to cover everyone's basic imperfections. A live fantasy world, disguising the reality that the primary reason this club was in business was to make money, and for the displaying of some flesh, some bare boobs and a pussy or two, would allow the dancers and management to separate the patrons from their hard-earned dollars. Some patrons with more mundane lives for which this was the most exotic, erotic thing they ever did, the money was a fair exchange. Everyone left happy. The end result was the American dream, commerce.

There were certainly some beautiful young women here tonight, maybe 100 women working in all, all sizes, ages, body types, ranging from goth girls with tats and multiple piercings to delicate innocent types who acted if they have never been in a club like this before.

The furnishings were large comfortable low back chairs on rollers, small tables arranged around a long high stage, with two smaller stages toward the back of the room. A curtained entrance was under a small neon sign reading "VIP". The music was surprisingly good, not so loud as to prevent conversation at the table. We ordered beers from the skinny waitress in the sequined black bustier.

I surveyed the half-full room, several girls clustered at the bar waiting for the crash of customers later in the night, an upscale group, many men in sport jackets, some of the girls in evening dresses, scattered around the room sitting on the laps of some of the patrons, playing the game of "buy me a drink and I'll stay here on your lap and chat with you." It was apparently a professional club with two thick necked bouncers in tuxes off to the side, watching the room carefully. There was not any groping or touching that I could see.

Two pretty young girls walked by, running their hand along the back of the seat and brushing my back at the same time, instinctively causing me to look up. "Hey baby, would you like some company?" they would ask.

"Not now," I would answer. After a while I noticed Aaron was texting again. He leaned over to me.

I need to ask an indulgence of you," he said. "Be cool. Roll with the evening. When Eleanor comes in, please don't run to her, do not make a scene, as it will not end well. Let her take the lead." He paused, staring at me. "I think you are in the right spot emotionally for this, but I am asking to please do not acknowledge she is your wife while here. Be only another guy in the room. You are indulging in her fantasy now." Aaron smiled is reassuring smile. "In other words hang back and don't fuck the evening up. I have confidence you can handle it. If you cannot, we'd best leave now and let them catch up with us back at the house."

"I'm good," I said, not as certain in my mind as I was in my words.

I wasn't sure why Aaron had chosen now to put the emphasis on my remaining calm until I looked up. Coming into the room were two broad shouldered very black men, imposing, confident, 6' 3" to 6' 4" I estimated, tight shirts outlining tight abs under sport jackets. Athletes at first glance, defensive end size. Between them was a gorgeous woman, blond hair with bangs over her forehead, a model face with smoky almost black around her eyes, makeup a tad thick, and bright red lipstick on her full lips, oversized hoop earrings framing her face.

She boasted a nice pair of boobs, the sides of which were visible through a totally sheer black shirt, a black and silver loose brocade vest covering all the good parts, but still sexy. She was wearing a pair of lace pants, all but sheer, a black thong clearly visible underneath. She was smiling, giddy, holding the thick arms of both men, making a head turning entrance. The hair color and heavy make-up threw me off for a milli-second, it was my wife, Eleanor.

"Damn," I heard Aaron say under his breath as he saw her. "Awesome."

"Damn's right," I added, watching as the scantily dressed woman approached up flanked by two massive black men. She smiled at Aaron, glanced at me with no recognition, save as they walked by, like the strippers earlier she ran her hand over the back of my seat, her fingers touching my back as if she had an electrical charge in her fingers.

I watched her pass, her bare ass exposed in the lace pants, only the string of the thong up the crack of her ass showing she was not totally naked under the pants. I was not the only one staring.

The trio was shown to a table with a reserved sign, a few rows back from the front, in the dim light outside the edge of the stage lights. They were three tables away from me, but situated in a way that I had a clear view.

The black men had their back to me, my wife was facing me. She locked eyes with me once for a fleeting second before staring at one of the black men, rising from her chair with her drink in hand and moving to his lap, at almost a side view to me.

The black man wrapped his arm around my wife, his hand sliding up under the vest, clearing copping a feel. She laughed and leaned over to give him a quick buss, wrapping her arm around his shoulder, talking to both him and the other man.

"That's Jerome," Aaron said. "I'll introduce you later."

As they finished their drinks, Eleanor shifted to the lap of the other black man, giving me a side view

134

from the other angle, and like Jerome, his hand too slid inside her vest to play with her tits. Eleanor made no move to stop the public display and was not discreet as I saw guys at a nearby table lean over and all heads there turned to see the beautiful woman with the two black men.

Another stripper came by, not asking, plopping down on my lap, observing my staring at the table with the two black men. "Hey," she said, "I'm not pushing for a drink or a dance, I just need somewhere to land for a second. An obnoxious pervert came in and he creeps me out—and he likes me, he says."

I did not object, and she looked over at their table. "Lucky girl," she said. "I'm Bridget." She extended her hand.

"You think?" I asked.

"Oh yeah, she's in for a good time tonight." I did offer to buy Bridget a drink, a vodka and cranberry, and she sipped it quietly, making small talk, "You're new here aren't you, I've not seen you before, I only work Thursdays, Fridays and Saturdays, I have a waitress job at a pub on the edge of town too, stop by and see me there sometime, hey, you're kinda cute and she trailed off into a never ending stream of consciousness banter that I tuned out. She was pretty, her hair a little stringy, too thin for my tastes, but a pretty face and talkative, very talkative. There was no need to attempt conversation, she never stopped.

One consolation was it did stop the parade of dancers come up in an unstoppable chain of girls soliciting dances. She sat with me for two more rounds, and I continued watching my wife swapping back and forth between the laps of her two large black lovers, their occasional feeling her up, her obvious delight in being in public with the three of them, after a while had me wondering what was next.

Bridget finally tired of talking, excused herself, and I saw my wife stand and leave the two men. She went through a door beside the stage that I assumed was the lady's restroom. I was shocked when the two men left their table and came to ours. Aaron did not introduce me a first, but they both acknowledged me with a courteous nod.

"Hey Aaron, how's it hanging man," Jerome said.

"What you been up too," Aaron asked.

"Fuck you wouldn't believe it," the other man said. I assumed he was Orneal. "That girl is something, a wild little slut for sure."

"A wild woman," Jerome said.

"Well fuck," Aaron said. "Tell me, you've had her since lunchtime."

"We let her pick the agenda for the day, told her to surprise us and we would try to make it happen," Jerome said. "So we started off going by my place and fucking her for couple of hours. That girl is borderline nympho."

"She sure likes it," Orneal added. They were talking as if I wasn't there, but I assume they knew I was the husband of the woman they were describing fucking, but if they knew, it didn't hold them back.

"We started off spit roasting her, switched, and then Jerome went first, I left them two of them in the room, he comes out and she's calling for me to come in there. I got my turn. I thought we'd take a break, but she was only getting started."

Eleanor took a shower, took some time to put on makeup, and come out in those hot clothes she's wearing now," Jerome said, with a grin. "She wanted to go to the adult bookstore." I sat upright in the seat and leaned forward, as did Aaron.

"Why?" Aaron asked.

"Girl wanted to try out the booths, so we did. I bought a handful of tokens, we found three booths to the side that were empty, and she told Orneal to go in the one on the right, and for me to go in the one on the left, and she would take the middle. Course you know how that works."

"I stick my cock through the hole, and she is sucking me good," Orneal says, "Using her hand at the base of my cock, and I was cumming in no time. I was weak kneed. I pulled my cock in, cleaned up with a towel, and squatted down and looked through the hole. The girl had her top off and was tweeting on Jerome's meat flute. I could see her tugging on her nipples while she was doing it, she was making little whimpering sounds and shit. She was flat ass getting off on it. I watched for second, buckled up, and stepped outside. I stood there at the door for a second, and there was this tall skinny black kid slid by me into the booth before I could stop him. Oh fuck, I thought. I waited around and Jerome come out."

"I did like Orneal did," Jerome said, "peeked through the hole, and Eleanor was sucking another cock on the other side. I thought Orneal was going for a second sucking, didn't think nothing about it

137

until I went outside and there stood Orneal. We both kinda shrugged, like, oh well, ya know?" It wasn't too long till the skinny kid comes out, sees Orneal still there and say, "Damn, that girl could suck a golf ball through a garden hose. That was one fantastic blow job." He had wandered away when the door opened and Eleanor came out, top and vest back on, wiping at her mouth with a paper towel. We went for a quick bite and she went into the ladies' room and reapplied her make up, came out and you would have no idea this fresh-looking white girl had sucked three different black cocks only minutes before."

***

I didn't speak, but my breath was coming in near pants now. I didn't consider whether this was something that surprised me, something I wished she had not done, or even surprised at her openness and boldness. I couldn't associate that the two black men talking about the slutty woman were talking about my wife. The only thought was the throbbing hard on I was trying to conceal. Right or wrong it was erotic and hot.

***

"Then?" Aaron asked.

"In a while," Jerome said, staring at the stage. The music changed and the DJ announced, "New favorite, Britney is here tonight. Give her a hand guys." There was only a smattering of applause, and

138

into the lights strode the blond with bangs. Britney was my wife. She had the same top and vest but had dropped the pants and only had the black thong on the bottom. I glared at Aaron.

"Oh, almost forgot," Aaron said, "Orneal, Jerome, this is Eleanor's husband, Brett."

"Oh fuck," Jerome said, "Sorry man, I wasn't paying attention, hope I didn't say anything offensive or nothing. Just telling the truth, understand?"

"It's all good," I said.

"Girl auditioned the other night, the manager offered her a job, and she took him up on it for tonight anyway. She said she wanted to show off for her husband," Jerome said. "That'd be you," he added, smiling a toothy grin.

Show off she did, strutting around the stage, swinging on the brass bar, stepping to the back and shrugging out of her vest, taking hard steps that caused her breasts to bounce under the sheer top, making one round like than, going to the back of the stage again and removing the top, turning to face the crowd, her arms crossed, palms covering her breasts, walking the length of the stage, leaning back on the pole and giving an overstated sly grin. She gave it a five count and spread her arms out, displaying her tits to the room, smiling, as if saying, "everyone take a look at my bare tits, they are out here for you."

Everyone's eyes were indeed riveted on the beautiful woman with the full tits on stage, with each nipple pierced with a small gold ring, glinting and reflecting in the bright stage lights.

"What the fuck?" I said aloud.

139

"What she wanted to do this afternoon," Jerome explained. "Her idea. Wanted to make tonight special, since it was the last night of the program," he said.

There was nothing to say. I sat there in stunned disbelief, the two black men sporting big smiles, Aaron watching, glancing over at me from time to time, and my wife proudly exhibiting her bare body on stage, the last song with her stripping off the thong and making a round. There was now a pile of bills littering the stage.

At each man who had laid a 20 in front of him at the front rail, she sat down on the stage, leaned back against the pole, and reaching down spread her pussy lips toward him. After the third time more twenties appear on the stage, each man getting the same reaction. The black men on the stage row were pointing at her pussy, and other black men moved to the stage and laid out their 20's.

I did not see until why until she spread her pussy in our direction for the guy in a direct line with us. On her pubis was a black spade with a Q inside. Her pussy was soaked, her juices glistening in the bright light of the stage lights. There was no concealing how turn on she was, displaying herself to this room full of strangers.

"Queen of spades, that tat on her pussy," Jerome explained, and he leaned toward me. "Means her pussy prefers black dick." I didn't believe my wife would mark herself like this. It was hard to comprehend that the woman I left off at lunch today, who had for the past week been my typical shy

140

spouse was now stripping on stage and proclaiming to the room that she loved black cock. It was too much.

I felt nauseous, I started to stand. Jerome put a meaty hand on my forearm. "Sit still Brother, like you said, it's all good. Don't mean it ain't a little shocking, but that will pass. Chill." If she had her nipples pierced what did it say about her frame of mind. I was clueless.

I sat back down, watching my naked wife gather up her clothes in a bundle and walk off stage. I looked up and all three men were looking at me for my reaction. I knew my face had broken out in a flush. No one spoke for a second. I do not know what reaction they were expecting, but from the look on their faces I didn't have the look they expected. They were all studying my reaction.

Jerome leaned over to me, gently laid his hand on my forearm and I turned to look at him. "I got to know the girl pretty good, you know she has done all this for you. She's wanting to show you how much she had shed her inhibitions, let her inner slut out." I had no comeback he was right. "Enjoy the hot slut you got now."

Aaron added, "Your wife's how you said you wanted her to be, now quit being a dick and enjoy the extraordinary gift she has given you, a woman who can let herself go like she has—and still go home with you in the end. She's never seen any other ending to this than going home with you."

"Speak of the devil," Orneal said. I looked up and my wife was approaching. Her vest was missing, she was holding her sheer top in her hand, again wearing the lace pants, bare breasted, weaving through the crowd, her breasts jiggling with each step. I stared transfixed as she approached, stunned at the gold nipple rings. I knew how sensitive her nipples were—to have done this?

My wife smiled at Aaron, leaned over and bussed me on the cheek, whispered "I love you," and moved back to Jerome's lap like before. "Hey guys, I can only stay a minute, one guy wants a table dance, and I have to do at least one before I go, boss man said. Just wanted to come over here and say don't leave without me." She handed me her sheer blouse. "Here, hold this honey. I think some bitch stole my vest."

Again she twisted away, topless, weaving through the crowd, every man's head turning as she walked by, stopping at a black man in a three piece business suit, taking a small stand the waitress bought, stepping on to it and began swaying to the beat, twisting in front of the man, close in between his legs, slowly twisting around in a circle as she danced, leaning over and pulling her finger over her thong covered pussy, twisting around again rubbing her tits in his face, pushing his hands away when he reached for them, teasing and laughing, sultry and enticing. I wanted her at that moment, as I suspect every man watching her. She was radiating sexuality and desire.

The song ended, the waitress retrieved the small stand, and again my topless wife returned to our table, unashamed, even proud, her shoulders back, smiling back at the appreciative stares, reveling in the attention. When she returned to the table she reached for the top, pulled it back on and buttoned it, although buttoned the top covered nothing, the nipple rings still reflecting in the room lights.

My wife didn't look at me directly, addressing Jerome and Orneal. "You guys about ready to go? I think I ready for some real partying."

"What you got in mind," Jerome asked.

My wife looked at me directly. "Me fucking and sucking two big black men," she said, pausing and smiling at me. "As my husband watches."

"Let's go," Aaron said.

We stood to leave, with Eleanor in the lead in her sheer blouse, I took up the rear, watching the stares and envious looks as she paraded by, anticipating what she had described.

"Come on, you ride with me," Aaron said. "Not room in Jerome's sports car." I watched my wife disappear to the other side of the parking lot between the two massive black men.

I leaned back in the seat as if sleepy to prevent further conversation, and to pull my thoughts together. Was this really happening to me?

143

Chapter 17

We arrived at Aaron's first, I followed him inside and sat in one easy chair facing the door while he made drinks. In about five minutes the door opened, Jerome and Orneal first, going straight to the couch, with my wife standing in the foyer. She removed the sheer blouse and the lace pants. I noticed she was no longer wearing her thong, and she stretched, her arms behind her head, smiling at us. She pulled the blond wig off her head, removing the pins and covering holding her hair, and shook her head, her black hair cascading down.

Aaron walked to her and whispered something. Eleanor looked confused at first before she opened the drawer on the foyer table and put on her wedding rings. Nude she walked toward the couch, standing in front of the two black men. "Looks like everyone is overdressed. Anyone wanting their cocks sucked better get them out here now."

Jerome and Orneal wasted no time, and I noticed Aaron unbuckling his pants too. Eleanor was beaming in anticipation of a room full of cocks to play with—and she turned to me. "That includes you baby, don't be the Lone Ranger here." She came over to me first and knelt down, reaching for my belt. "Here let me help you," she said, tugging down my unzipped pants and eagerly taking my cock in her mouth.

My wife has sucked my cock hundreds of times, but never like this. Maybe knowing we were being

144

watched added something to it, for sure the build up and watching my wife's sexy antics didn't hurt. I felt the coolness over her metal nipple rings on my thighs as she pressed her breasts into my leg. She only sucked my cock for a minute or so before stopping. "I'll finish with you later," she smiled, standing.

In turn she moved to Orneal, then Jerome, finishing off neither, explaining, "I'm saving your cum for a little later." Last in line was Aaron, who she sucked for a few minutes and ordered him to scoot down in the chair. His hands reached for her breasts, but she pushed him away. "Easy, they are very sore right now," she said, "but how about this?"

My wife straddled his lap and reaching down guided his cock into her pussy. I watched his cock disappear inside her and noticed that the Queen of spades tattoo on her pussy was chipping on the edge. It had been a rub on.

The descriptions I had heard from Aaron and the others of my wife's enthusiasm for fucking was on full display. I never recall her acting as if she needed and yearned for cock the way she was tonight, taking the lead, clearly it was Eleanor fucking Aaron, not the other way around. She was hungry for it. All he had to do was sit there as my wife impaled himself on his cock, faster and in rhythm to her soft grunts, coming more rapid. She was looking in his face.

"This is the last fuck from you through the program," she said, "come in me. Make it one you'll remember." The words triggered his orgasm. She ground down on his cock before pulling off, looking over at the two black men.

"Let's take this into the bedroom," she said, and they rose, following her, with my wife glancing over her shoulder at me. It was not a request when she said, "Come along, I don't think you want to miss this." As I looked down at the slate floor, I could see spots where Aaron's cum was dripping from my wife's pussy.

I glanced over at Aaron. "Enjoy," he said. "I'm going to sit here and recover." I followed the trio into the bedroom, where my wife was soon sandwiched between the two huge black men, kissing Jerome as Orneal fingered her pussy from behind, adding two, then three fingers into her pussy, causing her to kiss Jerome with more strength and passion. She turned back to Orneal, kissing him now as Jerome gently cupped her breasts from behind, carefully avoiding her newly pierced nipples, his hard cock on her back.

Eleanor gently pushed the two men to their backs, on her knees between them, stroking both cocks at one time, a cock in each hand, looking back and forth and pausing to suck one, then the other, both of their cocks thick and straight up erect.

Still on her hands and knees she released Jerome and Orneal. Orneal rose to his knees in front of her and Jerome was behind her, moving closer on his knees, his hand guiding his cock toward her pussy. As she felt the head of his cock touch her pussy, she shoved her body back onto to his cock. "Yesss," she hissed through closed teeth before pulling Orneal closer and sucking his cock back into her mouth, rocking back and forth on her knees.

Neither man had to move but remain stationary as my wife rocked back and forth on their cocks. Each slide back on to Jerome's cock pulled her mouth almost off Orneal's dick, and as she pulled off of Jerome's, the forward movement put Orneal's cock deep down her throat. She was moaning soft guttural grunts as she fucked. She came once like this that I could tell, tried to pull off Orneal's cock as she did but the two men held her in place until Orneal said, "switch" and the two men reversed position, twisting my wife around until it was Orneal's cock in her pussy and Jerome's in her mouth. Orneal was pumping her pussy in a hard steady rhythm, the balls making a slapping sound as the popped against her flesh.

"Get on your back," she told Orneal and he lay down. My wife straddled him, riding his cock while Jerome moved to her head, on his knees where she resumed sucking his cock, again they switched positions, and Orneal moved behind Eleanor, as if to stick his cock in either her ass or her pussy.

"Not tonight," she said, pushing his cock away. "I need some plain fucking."

Orneal moved away and Jerome rolled her to her back, pushing her knees up to her shoulders, looming over her. "Open them legs wide and let me take that white pussy, slut," he said.

"Yes, take my slutty cunt," she shot back, "my pussy loves big black cock."

Jerome was pounding her now. "Whose pussy is it?"

147

"It's your pussy, my cunt belongs to you, fuck me good baby. Put your black seed deep inside my pussy."

"You want that black seed?"

"Yes, fill my pussy full," Eleanor screamed, "Plant that black seed inside me."

"Gonna coat that womb right now," Jerome moaned and from the jerking of his muscles he was clearly cumming inside my wife. He held himself inside her pussy for a minute, then pulled out, rolling to the left.

Eleanor did not move from her position, looking at Orneal. "I'm in the breeding position," she said. "Breed me. My pussy wants another load of black baby juice," she told him. Orneal eagerly moved over her and pushed his cock into her.

Eleanor was almost trancelike in her passion, as if some uncontrollable force had taken over and was racking her body with orgasms, her chest flushed, her muscles tensing and releasing as the big cock pumped into her. "Fuck me, fuck me, fuck me," she was moaning to Orneal.

Orneal was large enough to fuck her in that position and kiss her at the same time, and she started cumming again, "I love how you fuck this white slut," she said. "Fuck your whore. You made me your whore when you paid for my pussy, fuck me good," she was moaning.

The bed was creaking, the room was smelling of sex, and the air was permeated with grunts and gasps. I looked closely at Eleanor's face, a mask of ecstasy but a tear rolling out of the corner of her eye from the intensity of the fucking.

Orneal was thrusting harder, deep. "Want my cum?" he grunted. "You want it in you or on you?"

"In me, deep in me," My wife moaned, shocking me with what she said next. "Knock me up Daddy, give me a black baby. Paint my womb with your cum."

Orneal gave a loud moan and he added his load to the other two loads of cum inside her, collapsing and rolling to the other side of my wife. She held her body up in that position for a moment before lowering her legs, cum pouring from her pussy. I watched it come out in round white globs until she lowered her hand to her crotch and felt it, running her forefinger through the mass of sperm. She lifted her cum coated finger to her mouth and licked it.

"I feel like I've just been fucked," she said.

"Last night here, wanna make it memorable," Eleanor said. She raised her head and looked at me. "Did you like that? You always said you wanted to watch."

I could only stammer a "Hell yes."

"Want to take a break," Jerome asked.

"For a minute, I need some water," Eleanor said. "You know when we started this, I thought I would fuck all four of you, turn this into a gangbang, but I don't think so now. I think more of my two black men is what I want instead." She again raised her head at me. "If you don't mind, head on home now, I'll be on a little later." I was being dismissed. She was clearly not through with the two black men.

I was almost in a daze, stunned and amazed at what I had witnessed. Aaron was fully dressed, with a drink waiting for me.

"Don't be offended, this is the last night," he said. "I suspect she wants you to think about what you have seen, process it, and be ready to talk when she gets home. Give her these last few hours."

"OK, I guess," I said, numbly polishing off the drink and stepping outside. "I have one question."

"Yes?"

"Is everything in your email today you described true?"

Aaron smiled, "I think you should let her answer." Aaron handed me a brown envelope. "Here, don't forget your calendar." I walked out the door and when I started the car, the clock said it was 1 a.m.

Chapter 18

I drove home, poured another drink, sat down in my recliner and did try to process what I had seen, how I had seen my beautiful wife acting tonight, and trying to put everything into the slots of what I expected, what I didn't expect, the shocking surprises, and what I anticipated for the future, and the looming question, the 700 pound gorilla in the room, how do Eleanor and I, and our marriage, survive this.

At some point the adrenaline on which I had been running all night faded away and I crashed into a deep sleep sitting in my recliner.

I was still asleep when my wife returning home woke me. I looked at the clock. Almost 6 a.m.

***

Eleanor took one look at me in the recliner, came over and kissed me on the forehead, whispered "poor baby, you relax here, I'll make us some coffee." I heard her rattling around in the kitchen and smelled the coffee brewing. I tried to rouse myself, going to the upstairs bathroom, washing my face, changing my clothes from the night before into casual sweats and a tee shirt, my usual lay around the house uniform.

Eleanor had done basically the same thing downstairs, wearing her thin hot-tub robe.

151

"How about we pour some Jameson in the coffees and take this to the hot tub," I suggested.

"Let's," she smiled.

"Let me get my trunks," I said.

"We won't need them, come on," she said, letting the robe slide off her shoulders, and nude boldly walking into the yard to the hot tub, folding the cover back, and climbing in. I was right behind her, the rest of the coffee in an insulated urn and the freshly opened bottle of Jamie.

"Oh that feels good," she said as the heat hit her. "I have muscles stretched and flexed that I didn't know I had." She was as nonchalant as she had been throughout this program, but now there was no program. She caught herself. "OK, where do you want me to start?"

***

I studied her, my beautiful wife, looking the same as when this started, same loving warm smile, same scrubbed look without makeup, no one the wiser of these past eight weeks, except the two gold hoops in her nipples—and what I had witnessed.

"The narrative that Aaron sent?"

"I read it. All true. I had those fantasies, he convinced me it was important that I live them," she said. "I felt free enough to consider living my fantasies for the first time, so I did."

"Was it important?"

"Yes. For me anyway. I hope it didn't hurt you or stress you out too much," Eleanor said.

152

"Just a lot to have hit me at one time," I said.

"And what would you change about what has happened? Which fantasy would you have not wanted me to live? Would you take back any, including any of your fantasies?" she asked.

The question set me back. I had been in a snit, feeling as if I had been blindsided with all the different men my wife had fucked, the boldness and open slutty behavior she had exhibited, but would I change any of it?"

"You tell me? Would you change any of it?" I asked.

"You always accuse me of answering a question with a question, but I give. I've had time to think about this as each step happened, and each time I chose to continue, each time I came up with a new fantasy I wanted to enjoy, to try. So I did. You wanted me out of my shell. I'm out. You wanted me more forward, I am. You wanted me confident in myself. I'm that too. You wanted me slutty, but you never said the words, but I've read some of the things on your computer and picked up on your hints, and I am, I'm a slut, I've been a whore," Eleanor said, pausing, "And if that is too much for you, I understand, I did get out of control there for a while. I surprised myself. But there is no going back either. We cannot go back to exactly the way we were."

"I still love you, I cannot change that, nothing has changed that," I said.

"And I love you," she said. "The question is can you still love me, and live with me, knowing what

153

you know, without it eating you up inside? Without regret to what I did?"

I looked into her eyes, other than her moving much farther along that I thought she would go, I did not want to let her get away. "It will not eat me up," I said, and even as I said it the formula for the future evolved out in my mind. "But that may mean you will have to replay it in your mind, describe to me what you felt as it was happening."

Eleanor saw through me, smiling. "So you are glad you have slut wife now?"

"I guess so." I said surrendering, "I have one either way, so I'm good." She had a satisfied smile. "One question."

"There will be more than one, I know, but go ahead."

"Aaron, Jerome, Orneal, all bareback?"

"Yes, Aaron and Jerome showed me tests. When Orneal picked me up streetwalking I made him use a condom, and the other guy I made use a condom, and Eric, from the wedding when I bumped into him. I did get carried away with Orneal when we got back after the whoring episode, but he has since been tested so it was all good."

"And the talk about wanting a black baby?"

"Pillow talk only, shit that both of them got off on. You know that isn't going to happen," she said, pausing to study my face before adding, with a taunt, "but it is kinda hot, don't you think?"

"Yeah, just after the last child leaves home, you want to joke about that?"

154

"Well biracial babies are sooo cute," My wife said, pausing, seeing my face. "I'm joking, you know that." She kept a stone face for only a moment before breaking into a laugh. "Gotcha."

"How do you see this going forward, where do you want to go with it?" I asked.

"I want to make you happy; I want to be happy; I want us to enjoy life together," she said. "I am not sure if occasionally fucking someone else would interfere with that or not, I think that would depend on you."

"I think I'm good if I can watch," I admitted. "Last night was the most erotic thing I've ever seen."

"That can be arranged," Eleanor laughed. "I've discovered I'm something of an exhibitionist, so I enjoy you watching me. I thought that was very hot, performing for you. It was." Again, a pause, she was thinking. "Do you mind if they all my sexual partners would be black?" I raised my eyebrows in a questioning look. "You know what they say, once you go black," my wife said. "It's true with me."

"We're outlining a map here aren't we, a map for going forward?"

"I guess so," she said. "You have veto power you know."

"As do you," I said. "So how do you see hooking up? I trust you are through streetwalking?"

"Some fantasies are one and done," she laughed. "Like that, and like sucking cocks in a glory hole. Damn that was so nasty."

"Stripping?"

155

"I don't think I'd take that off the table. It's not like at my age I could do that long term, I guess a lot would depend on what you thought about it. I'm 50-50 on it."

"Let's table that for the moment, come back to it later."

"As for hooking up, bars are fun, but only as a contact. Don't forget I have three black men's phone numbers that caught my interest there, a half dozen men from the online sites I set up, and I think you saw that Jerome and Orneal are ready any time I am. When I want to, I think it is a matter of picking who is going to get lucky, don't you?"

"Apparently," I said.

"So we are good?" I asked.

"Yes, I think we are," she said, "other than a good welcome home fuck. I want a good fuck from my husband, with him knowing now I'm a slut and a whore."

"What I've waited for," I said. She came into my arms, kissed me, backing away with an "ouch" when her nipples hit my chest. "Sorry, very tender still."

"You like those?" I asked.

"I think I will. I surprised you with that too, didn't I?"

"You have surprised me in a hundred different ways, all good now that you are here," I said.

"I'll always be here baby. Now come fuck me. Be easy though, I got used pretty hard last night." She saw my face and laughed. "Yeah I know you, I douched before I left, I had a ton of black cum inside me, I would have been dripping for days if I hadn't."

156

She kissed me again, broke the kiss and breathed in my ear, "I want my pussy full of your white cum, my husband. Let's go do it."

"Let's," I grinned, following her inside.

***

It was when I checked my email the first time after Eleanor's return that I saw one from Aaron. What this time? I thought. I opened it.

"Brett, I forgot to mention in addition to the calendar in the brown envelope, there is a thumb drive with some videos of some of the better parts of the sessions. As you can imagine some are better lit than others, depending on the circumstance. I thought the video might be more revealing than my descriptions. I didn't tell Eleanor the videos existed until she left, I was afraid if she knew she was being filmed it would have inhibited her. (Permission to film her was in a sub-paragraph on the contract).

Also despite the program making substantial changes in both of you, I do hold a refresher weekend at my place in Macon, or sometimes at the beach, just to keep the training in mind. You would be on hand for everything during the refresher. I think it is fair to say Eleanor would get fucked a lot though.

Yes, some call what we did "wife training" but it has such a negative connotation and does not accurately describe the program, we prefer to call it the "program." You would have balked had I told you I planned to train your wife, but it is what it is.

157

And I suspect that now you two can openly discuss your fantasies. I'd bet that your wife has a few that she still hasn't revealed. Stay well and enjoy.

***

Thus prompted I let weeks separate us from the end of the program before I brough it up. It was exceptional hot sex as I had watched my wife on the video dressed as a hooker, twisting her ass on the street as a silver Escalade pulled up, watching her lean in the window before climbing in and disappearing around the corner. The audio was still on as I saw their view from that night, and heard Jerome saying, "Oh fuck, that's Orneal now, who the fuck was in the other Escalade?"

Aaron give an exasperated, "Oh shit. At least she is with Orneal now and safe."

***

"What other fantasies do you have?" I asked my wife, once she felt able to open up about the program.

"You mean any fantasies that I do not mention because I might want to live them?" she said.

"Yes."

"I don't know. I'll let you know," she said. "I have been thinking about a real tat though."

"Oh," I said, without asking what she had in mind. I had a pretty good idea already.

"What about you, you have any unspoken fantasies? Regrets at what has happened? We do not get do overs, remember," Eleanor said.

"I can't think of any at the moment," I said. "If I do, I'll let you know—before we attend the refresher weekend."

***

And this is how I ended up laying on the beach on St. Martin eight months later, nude. My wife who had in our prior visit to Orient beach insisted on bashfully staying on her chaise lounge, took a different approach today. She stood up, stretched her nude body and smiled down at me. "Come on baby, walk me down the beach. Show your hotwife off."

Which is how I ended up spying a nice silver waist chain made for decorating an otherwise nude woman, haggling with the seller, following the beautiful naked woman now a distance away, further up the beach, smiling at the young black man with dreads and a thick swinging cock approaching her.

As she had asked the year before, I had brought her back here—and yes, I am amazed at her change.

THE END